How important is winning?

Christina kept herself still in the saddle now, knowing that Callie was giving everything he had. The pounding of his strides accelerated as he powered toward the leaders.

One-two-three. One-two-three. One-two-three. One—

Suddenly Christina lurched in the saddle. The next galloping beats were jolting, making Christina's teeth clatter together.

Instinctively Christina pulled back on the reins, wanting to be sure that Callie was not hurt. Callie shook his head, fighting the restraint.

"Whoa, boy. Let's slow down, okay?" Christina gave the reins another tug.

Callie ignored Christina. He continued running with rough but strong strides, accelerating until he was almost even with the other horses.

Christina tried to check Callie's strides for lameness, but the colt's agitation was adding to the unevenness of his gait. She couldn't tell what the cause of this rough gallop was. Christina started to pull back on the reins again, but the continuing strength of Callie's strides made her hesitate. Was she willing to ruin Callie's chances of winning this race when she couldn't be sure that he was hurt?

Collect all the books in the Thoroughbred series

Collect all the books in the Ashleigh series

*coming soon

THOROUGHBRED

WIN A
FREE SADDLE!
SEE DETAILS
IN BACK.

TAKING
THE REINS

CREATED BY

JOANNA CAMPBELL

WRITTEN BY

JENNIFER CHU

HarperEntertainment
An Imprint of HarperCollinsPublishers

To Barbara, Charlene, Cindy, Dominique, Marisa,
and Patrick in honor of all our undergrad adventures

■ HarperEntertainment
An Imprint of HarperCollins*Publishers*
10 East 53rd Street, New York, NY 10022-5299

This is a work of fiction. The characters, incidents, and dialogues are
products of the author's imagination and are not to be construed
as real. Any resemblance to actual events or persons, living
or dead, is entirely coincidental.

▓ Produced by 17th Street Productions,
an Alloy Online, Inc., company

HarperCollins books are available at special quantity discounts for bulk
purchases for sales promotions, premiums, or fund-raising.
For information please call or write:
Special Markets Department, HarperCollins Publishers Inc.,
10 East 53rd Street, New York, NY 10022-5299.
Telephone: (212) 207-7528. Fax: (212) 207-7222.

ISBN 0-06-054440-6

Cover art © 2003 by 17th Street Productions,
an Alloy Online, Inc., company

First printing: August 2003

Printed in the United States of America

Visit HarperEntertainment on the World Wide Web at
www.harpercollins.com

❖ 10 9 8 7 6 5 4 3 2

From a distance, the racetrack at Belmont Park looked like a place in a fairy tale. The morning sunlight hit the racetrack's outer railings at such an angle that the white paint glowed. Within these railings, a dirt track stretched so far, it seemed that if the horses ran fast enough, they might be able to touch the sky. The surrounding ivy-covered buildings and tall, leafy trees complemented the track, giving it a dreamlike appearance.

Upon closer examination, though, the track lost its peaceful beauty. Socialite spectators, dressed in dark-colored business suits or pastel sundresses, crowded around the lawn. Bettors screamed into their cellular phones as they paced the grandstands and stuffed money under the betting windows. This chaos extended to the backside, where trainers, grooms, veterinarians, race stewards, and reporters milled around, inspecting horses and barking orders.

Christina Reese tried to ignore the commotion as she stood in front of Wonder's Star's stall and answered questions from the press. Two months earlier, such attention would have rattled her. But this day her responses came easily.

"Ms. Reese, what's next for Wonder's Star?"

Christina looked at her racehorse, admiring the chestnut colt's rippling muscles, straight legs, and elegant head. "Well, first of all, he's going home to Kentucky to get some well-deserved rest," she replied, rubbing the white whorl on Star's forehead. "After that, we'll probably bring him to Saratoga."

"Is the Travers Stakes a possibility?"

Christina nodded. She was planning to enter Star in the biggest race of the Saratoga meet. "But it's not definite. We want to keep our options open." Her parents, Mike Reese and Ashleigh Griffen, were standing at the front of the audience. They had warned her to keep her answers conservative.

"What about the Breeders' Cup Classic?"

Ashleigh stepped forward. "That's certainly on our minds, but we don't want to get too far ahead of ourselves," she replied.

Christina's mind wandered as her mother discussed Star's summer and fall schedule, listing races such as the Jockey Club Gold Cup. She looked toward the racetrack, remembering the moment that had changed her life just days ago.

It's Wonder's Star! Wonder's Star wins the Belmont!

Finally, after being boxed in during the Kentucky Derby and bumped during the Preakness Stakes, Christina and Star had come back to win the last leg of the Triple Crown, the mile-and-a-half Belmont Stakes, by a length. Since Star's difficult birth, Christina had known he was special enough to win a Triple Crown race. The path certainly hadn't been easy, but now she and Star had finally shown the racing world what they were capable of.

Ashleigh touched Christina's shoulder. Blushing, Christina turned her attention back to the reporters. A woman in the back was asking a question.

"Christina, now that you have graduated from high school, what are your plans for the future?"

Christina suppressed a groan. Lately it seemed as though everyone was asking her that question. She still didn't have the answer. Back in February she had been accepted to the University of Kentucky in Lexington. Wanting to focus on Star, she had convinced her parents to let her defer admission for a year. Then, as the Triple Crown races drew closer, she had begun thinking about postponing college even longer to focus on her career as a jockey.

Lately, though, the people she respected had found reasons for her to give college more serious consideration. Cindy McLean, a close family friend who had been a successful jockey at Belmont before an injury forced her retirement, had insisted that a solid knowledge of business was necessary for any career with horses. Meanwhile, Christina's ex-boyfriend Parker Townsend had proven it was possible to work with horses while going to school. Finally, Star's groom, Dani Martens, had gotten Christina interested in the possibility of veterinary school.

"I'm not sure about my next step right now," Christina told the reporter. "All I know is that I will continue working with Star."

During the Triple Crown it had been hard for Christina to think about anything beyond the Belmont Stakes. The competition had been so intense that all she'd been able to focus on was Star's next race. But now Star was getting a break, and it was time to make it on her own as a jockey. She was planning to stay at Belmont for the rest of the meet, even though her parents and Star were leaving for Kentucky that evening. Ian McLean, the head trainer at Whitebrook, her parents' farm, would be supervising the farm's horses at Belmont. Ian had several promising horses for Christina to ride.

Christina answered a few more questions for the reporters, but that one reporter's question kept echoing in her head.

What *did* she want to do with her life? How much of her love for jockeying came from her love for Star and how much would remain if she was riding other horses? Were Cindy, Parker, and Dani right about college? Or should she wait until she was sure before she enrolled? In the meantime, what was the best way for her to spend the summer? There were so many questions, and Christina didn't have any answers.

As the crowd dissipated she left Star's stall and walked along the backside, wanting some time to think. The sound of a familiar voice calling her name interrupted Christina's thoughts. Turning, she saw Patrick and Amanda Johnston walking toward her. In April Christina had taken Star to the Johnstons' Dreamflight Racing Farm in California so that she could race her colt in the Santa Anita Derby. She had heard from the famous West Coast trainers only a few times since then.

"Hi, Christina. How are you?" Amanda greeted her. Amanda was wearing a long yellow sundress, and her blond hair was tied back with a matching yellow silk scarf. Christina had never understood how the trainer could spend so much time around horses yet look so put together. Christina herself usually went around the track in ratty jeans, and no matter how hard she tried to keep her auburn hair out of the way, the reddish strands still came loose and got in her face.

"Hi, Amanda. I'm doing fine," Christina replied politely. Even though she had stayed at Dreamflight for two weeks, she still didn't feel completely comfortable around the trainers. Before the Triple Crown they had given her a mount on Calm Before the Storm, one of their star horses, for the Lafayette and San Felipe Stakes. But they had nearly replaced her before the latter race because the colt had started struggling in his training. "How long have you been at the track?"

"We got in just before the Belmont," Patrick said. He was wearing khaki pants and a striped polo shirt, but since his shirt wasn't tucked in and his brown hair wasn't combed, he looked far more casual than his wife. "By the way, congratulations on your win. Star looked like a completely different horse from the one you brought to Dreamflight."

"He's come a long way," Christina said proudly. Before the Santa Anita Derby she had attempted to change Star's racing style, trying to get him to be a front-runner instead of a late closer, with disastrous results. For the Belmont she had followed the advice of Jean Cruguet, jockey of the former Triple Crown winner Seattle Slew, and had just hung on and let Star run the race his way. The outcome had been much better. "How's Callie?"

The Johnstons had wanted to race Calm Before the Storm in the Preakness, but a strained tendon had kept him off the Triple Crown trail. "He's faster than ever," Amanda answered, brushing some dirt off her sundress. "Aaron's riding him in the Riva Ridge Breeders' Cup this Saturday."

Christina smiled. At the end of her trip to California she had been able to convince Aaron Evans, one of Dreamflight's exercise riders, to test for his jockey's license. Aaron had passed and had ridden in half a dozen races so far. "Do you still want Callie to try distance races?" Christina asked. She had jockeyed the horse to victory in the San Felipe Stakes, which was a mile and a sixteenth. The Riva Ridge was only seven furlongs.

"Yes, but we wanted his first race after his injury to be a sprint," Amanda said. "Are you going to be here on Saturday?"

Christina nodded. "I plan to stay for the rest of the meet." She tried not to squirm under Amanda's gaze. Right after the San Felipe Stakes the Johnstons had talked about giving her more mounts. Did they still want her to ride for them?

"Would you be interested in riding one of our fillies, Noble Answer, in the Vagrancy Handicap, then?" Amanda offered. "She's still pretty skittish, and I'd prefer a jockey with more experience than Aaron."

"Of course I would," Christina replied quickly, unable to stop a grin from spreading across her face. "Do you want me to exercise her beforehand?"

"Sure. She and Callie will be arriving this afternoon, and we'll probably give them tomorrow off. Meet us on the track Wednesday morning," Patrick said. "We can probably rustle up a few more horses for you if you're interested." He looked over at Amanda, who nodded. "Actually, if Aaron's flight out of Los Angeles is delayed for more than another half hour, we'll need someone to ride Blue Streak this afternoon."

Christina considered for a moment. She remembered the rambunctious two-year-old gray colt and would have enjoyed the challenge. But she had already made plans for the afternoon, wanting to spend time with Parker before he left New York. Ever since her senior prom she and Parker had been dancing around the idea of getting back together. They needed to figure out once and for all whether they had a chance.

"Christina?" Amanda prompted. "Do you want the ride?"

"I do, but unfortunately, I'm busy this afternoon," Christina said, looking away. Accommodating the Johnstons was important if she wanted them to give her more mounts, but she had already sacrificed her relationship with Parker for her jockeying career once. She didn't want to make the same mistake again. "But I think my cousin, Melanie Graham, would be a great jockey for Blue Streak."

Christina was pleased by how easily that recommendation came out. Until recently Christina and Melanie's friendship had been strained because of the Triple Crown. Melanie had spent the last winter and spring working with her own Triple Crown hopeful, Perfect Image. Image had won the Kentucky Derby by two lengths, but the beautiful black filly had broken her left foreleg at the end of the race. Fortunately, surgery on the leg had been successful, and Image was now recovering at Townsend Acres, a rival racing farm in Kentucky. Image's injury had helped both Melanie

8

and Christina realize that there were more important things than winning. As the Belmont approached, they had finally put aside their differences and become friends again.

"Melanie's the jockey who won the Kentucky Derby, right?" Patrick again exchanged glances with his wife.

"And she also came in second in the Belmont on Gratis," Christina added. Gratis belonged to Ben al-Rihani of Tall Oaks, where Cindy McLean was the head trainer.

"Where can we find her?" Amanda asked.

"She was over at the Whitebrook stalls in barn nine when I left," Christina said. "I'm sure she'd be happy to ride for you."

Christina exchanged a few more polite remarks with the Johnstons before they walked away. Watching them leave, Christina returned to her previous train of thought.

As she considered her future Christina couldn't help feeling a little envious of her cousin. Unlike her, Melanie knew that she didn't want to be in school any longer. All Mel had wanted to do since she'd arrived at Whitebrook five years earlier was to be a jockey. Christina wished for that certainty. But now she was finally getting the chance to try the life of a jockey. That would make her decision easier, wouldn't it?

• • •

9

By early afternoon the grandstands were filled with people. Christina and Parker sat in the bleachers, watching the post parade for the first race, Blue Streak's maiden race. Parker would be leaving for the airport in just two short hours to return to Kentucky.

Christina turned to Parker and flushed when she realized that he had been staring at her. His smoky gray eyes burned into her hazel ones. "What?" she asked softly.

Parker smiled, and the harsher features on his face, including his stubborn jawline, loosened. "You're beautiful."

Christina looked away. "No, I'm not," she mumbled.

Parker took her hand, pulling her back to face him. "I've been thinking that we might have made a mistake in April."

Christina took a deep breath. April was when she and Parker had decided that they would end up hurting each other if they kept dating. Between Parker's goal of making the Olympic three-day event team and her dream of winning Triple Crown races with Star, they just hadn't had enough time for each other.

Were things any different now? Parker had come back from England, where he had been training for Burghley, a big autumn competition, so that he could watch the Triple Crown. But he would be flying back across the ocean soon. Meanwhile, Christina was probably going to spend her summer at Belmont and

Saratoga. This was the last time they'd see each other for months.

Parker rubbed Christina's hand with shaking fingers. "I thought it would be easier to push you away. But I'm still in love with you, Christina Reese."

Despite her doubts, Christina couldn't help admitting, "I'm still in love with you, too."

"Then we have to try again," Parker said, setting his jaw determinedly. He ran his free hand through his dark hair, a gesture he often repeated when he was thinking about serious matters. "Maybe we just need to be more realistic about how much free time we have."

Christina smiled ruefully. "Have you ever wondered what life would be like for us if we were normal?" she asked.

"What's so great about normal?"

Christina shrugged. "I spent most of my high school years working with Star. Sometimes I wonder whether I should have spent more time being a teenager instead of a jockey." Christina thought back to the weeks before graduation. Only then had she realized how far she had drifted from her good friends.

"What you've done with Star is incredible." Parker put his arms around her, holding her close.

Christina rested her head against his strong shoulder, realizing how much she had missed this. "Thank you," she whispered. "I know I shouldn't be complaining. I got a chance that most people never have. But I

11

want things to be less complicated—at least for us."

Parker pulled back, holding Christina at arm's length. "It's not complicated for me. I'd rather be with you part of the time than not be with you at all."

Christina felt tears spring to her eyes at those simple words. She swallowed, trying to keep her emotions under control. "So would I."

Parker kissed her forehead, a wide smile spreading across his face. His gray eyes brightened. "I'm going to miss you this summer," he said softly, running a finger down Christina's cheek.

Christina put her arms around him, burying her face in his neck. "I'm going to miss you, too." She closed her eyes tightly, still trying to hold back tears.

Parker rubbed her back. "But October will be here before we know it, and then I'll have the chance to give you that tour of the University of Kentucky campus that I promised you."

"Let's not talk about college right now."

Parker nodded before pressing his lips to her hair. "I know you'll make the right choices," he told her. "Hey, you just decided to give me another chance, didn't you?"

Christina's tension released itself in laughter. "That wasn't a hard decision."

"You'll figure it out," Parker said. "And either way, you're still looking forward to this summer, right?"

Christina nodded. "The only thing that could make it better is if you could be here." She paused. "But I know that's not fair. Training with Jack Dalton is a once-in-a-lifetime chance."

"Maybe you can fly over for Burghley," Parker suggested. "And no matter what, there's always the phone. I want to know everything that goes on at Belmont and Saratoga."

"Everything?"

"Everything. And I'll tell you everything about England." Parker put a hand under Christina's chin, slowly tilting her head up so that they could kiss. The kiss was long and sweet, and when Christina finally pulled back, Parker cupped her face with his hands. "I'm not saying the next few months are going to be easy, Chris. But remember that I love you, even when you're too busy to notice."

2

"AND DOWN THE STRETCH THEY COME! IT'S A THREE-HORSE race between First and Ten, Crossing Twilight, and Blue Streak. First and Ten holds a narrow lead. . . ."

Melanie could feel nervous energy shooting through the gray colt she was riding. Blue Streak hated running in a crowd. He had already snaked his head around and tried to bite another horse twice.

Melanie kneaded her fists along Blue Streak's neck, soothing him with her voice. "Easy, boy. Easy. We only have a little more to go." She glanced to either side, seeing the noses of the other horses. Fortunately, both of them were drifting wide, giving Blue Streak more room.

Melanie tapped Blue Streak with her crop, encouraging him to run. Blue Streak snorted, darting to the inside. Melanie corrected him with pressure from her left leg. "It's okay, Blue Streak," she murmured, trying to calm her mount with a singsong cadence. "Just run straight. Straight, good. Sideways, bad." She asked the colt for more speed with her legs and seat.

Blue Streak snorted again. He lowered his head, powering forward.

"Attaboy!" Melanie praised. Blue Streak was finally turning his tension into speed. His strides were strong and sure against the hard surface, pounding an even, determined rhythm. Melanie closed her eyes for a second, appreciating this rhythm. After the Kentucky Derby, she knew, she would never take it for granted again.

But the thought of the Kentucky Derby threw Melanie into a cold panic. The ground seemed to lurch before her, and she opened her eyes before she could relive the feeling of Image going down. "Come on, Blue Streak," she said, reminding herself that this was not the Kentucky Derby and that, despite the horrible accident, Image was going to be fine. She hit Blue Streak's shoulder with her crop. The gray colt leaped forward, crossing the finish line.

"Blue Streak wins it by a head over First and Ten!" the announcer cried.

Melanie stood in her stirrups, briefly waving her crop in victory. She hoped the Johnstons would be happy with her riding. As she eased Blue Streak to a jog the scenes from the end of the Kentucky Derby again threatened to invade her mind. Melanie ruthlessly pushed them aside. Image was still alive. The beautiful, headstrong black filly would never race again, but she was alive.

Melanie leaned down to praise Blue Streak as an outrider came over to get them. "Good job, boy. Did you like your first race? Next time maybe you should concentrate more on running instead of biting other horses." She rubbed the colt's neck. "You certainly kept me on my toes today."

In the winner's circle Melanie thanked the Johnstons for giving her the chance to ride and told them how well Blue Streak had responded down the stretch.

Amanda patted the colt. "He looks like he could run that race all over again. Patrick and I are thinking of entering him in an allowance next. Would you like to ride him?"

Melanie hesitated. She was going back to Kentucky with Aunt Ashleigh and Uncle Mike that evening so that she could work with Image. She planned to come back to Belmont soon, but she hadn't yet figured out her return date. Still, she didn't want to turn the Johnstons down. Now that high school was over, she needed such offers to jump-start her jockeying career. "When are you thinking about racing him?"

"About two weeks from now," Amanda replied.

Melanie was surprised. Her aunt and uncle liked to give their horses, especially the younger ones, more time between races. "I'm not sure whether I'll be back at the track by then," she said. "Can I give you an answer at the end of the week?" Image was scheduled to start walking on soft ground on Thursday. If the filly did well, it would be easier for Melanie to come back to Belmont.

"That's fine," Patrick said. He took Blue Streak's reins from Jessica, the colt's groom. "Now smile for the picture."

Later that evening Melanie was tearing around her bedroom at her father's house, trying to gather all her belongings. She usually traveled lightly, but coming to New York required her to pack nicer clothes for the various parties and social functions her father, a record producer, and his wife, Susan, liked to attend.

As she grabbed a handful of items off the bathroom counter, Melanie checked her reflection in the mirror. Her father and Susan were taking her out to dinner before she left for the airport, and she was a mess. Her short blond hair was still wet from the shower, and it clung lifelessly to her head. Melanie pulled a brush through the unruly layers before hurrying back to the bedroom.

The phone rang. Melanie jumped for it, figuring that it was her father. "Hi, Dad," she said as she picked it up. She rested the phone against her shoulder, trying to fold her clothing while she talked. "Don't worry if you're late. I haven't finished—"

"Mel?"

The phone slid off her shoulder. Melanie caught it in her right hand and sat down on her bed, abandoning the packing efforts. "Hi, Jazz."

Jazz Taylor was the lead singer of the popular band Pegasus. He was also Image's owner, and recently he had become Melanie's boyfriend.

"You must be in a hurry if you're talking before you figure out who's on the phone," Jazz teased.

"I'm sorry," Melanie apologized quickly. "I was packing, and I—"

"It's all right, Mel," Jazz interrupted. "I know you've been busy. I just wanted to let you know that I'm in Kentucky. I've managed to clear the days before our Friday concert in Lexington for my two girls."

"Two? Who's the other one?" Every time Pegasus played, dozens of girls followed Jazz around, squealing as they begged for autographs.

"Well, my main gal is a flighty, expensive one named Perfect Image, and I forget the name of the other one. Melanie something or other."

Melanie laughed, feeling silly about her momentary jealousy. "How is Image?"

"She looks better," Jazz replied. "She's gained back some of the weight that she lost after her surgery, and she loves that therapy pool. Dr. Dalton is very happy with her progress."

"Did Brad talk to you when you stopped by?" Melanie asked. The rivalry between her family and

Brad Townsend, the owner of Townsend Acres, stretched back over twenty years. Brad was ruthlessly competitive, and he always seemed to go out of his way to make life difficult for Aunt Ashleigh and Uncle Mike. After the Kentucky Derby Brad had mysteriously offered Townsend Acres' surgery and rehabilitation facilities to Image, effectively saving the filly's life. Melanie had started thinking that maybe he was a nicer, more generous person than her relatives believed. But Brad's recent displays of temper, especially after his prized colt, Celtic Mist, had come in third to Star and Gratis in the Belmont Stakes, suggested otherwise.

"No, but I received the latest bill a few days ago," Jazz said. "I have to be honest with you, Mel. The costs are already twice as high as the initial estimate Brad gave me."

Melanie was silent. She listened to the sound of Jazz's breathing on the other end of the line as she tried to come up with a response. On one hand, she didn't want to strain Jazz's financial resources. On the other hand, she knew that moving Image back to Whitebrook too early could compromise the filly's recovery.

There was another alternative, though. Brad had been hinting that he would accept ownership of Image's first foal as payment for the filly's surgery and rehabilitation. But Melanie wasn't quite ready to discuss that possibility.

"It's not anything to panic about yet," Jazz reassured her. "I'm probably worrying about nothing. The start of a tour always makes me worry about money. I'll be fine after we play a few concerts. Speaking of which, we just wrote a new song."

"What's it called?" Melanie allowed him to change the subject, even though it did little to ease her concerns. Sometime soon she and Jazz would have to consider giving Brad Image's first foal.

"'Long Shot.' Guess who inspired it."

Melanie smiled. Image had been a 20-to-1 long shot in the Kentucky Derby. "Why don't you sing it for me now?"

"You'll have to wait until Friday. I want it to be a surprise."

Melanie heard the front door opening. "I have to go, Jazz. Dad's home, and I still need to pack before dinner. I'll see you at Townsend Acres tomorrow morning, right?"

"Right. I can't wait to see you, Mel."

As Melanie hung up the phone she heard a knock at the door. "Come in," she called.

Christina stepped into her room. "Your father's downstairs. He sent me up to see if you needed any help taming this mess." She gestured to the piles of clothing on the floor.

"Definitely," Melanie said. She pushed a suitcase in her cousin's direction. "Just shove as much as you can in there. I don't care if anything gets wrinkled."

Christina nodded, sitting down beside one of the piles and quietly following instructions.

Melanie looked at her cousin more closely. Christina's face was pale, and her eyes were red. "You all right?"

"Yeah," Christina replied listlessly.

"Oh, I know you better than that. What's wrong?"

"I talked with Parker today."

For days Melanie had been pushing Christina to tell Parker how she felt. Now she wondered whether she had done the right thing. "What did he say?"

Christina lowered her head, mumbling her response. "We got back together."

"That's great!" Melanie exclaimed, but Christina didn't look up. "Aren't you happy?"

"I am. It's just that he left for the airport an hour ago. I probably won't see him for the rest of the summer." Christina bit her lip.

Melanie crossed the room, giving Christina a hug. "I'm sorry."

Christina shook her head. "There's nothing to be sorry about. I just have to face the fact that it'll be a while before we have time for each other." She shrugged. "I wish there were some way to make it all easier."

Melanie thought about what she could expect from her relationship with Jazz this summer. She would divide her time between Kentucky and Belmont. Meanwhile, Jazz would be busy touring with Pegasus on the East Coast, and the band would be playing in Europe for most of July. Maybe she could share her own long-distance relationship issues with Christina later. Now didn't seem like the right time. "Well, if anyone can make it, it will be you and Parker," Melanie said at last. "You two have been disgustingly cute together ever since Star was born."

"I can't even remember what my life was like back then," Christina replied. She resumed packing. "It seems like forever since I used to event."

Christina had ridden with Parker on the three-day event circuit at the beginning of high school. But Star's birth had convinced Christina to change her focus from eventing to racing. Melanie was willing to bet that if Christina had stayed focused on eventing, her cousin would be just as good as Parker was now.

"You're so lucky, Mel," Christina continued. "You always knew you wanted to be a jockey."

"But you know that now." Melanie couldn't imagine Christina wanting to do anything else after her Belmont win.

"I thought I did," Christina corrected her. "But I can't bring myself to rule out college or veterinary medicine."

In the weeks before the Belmont Christina had been toying with the idea of becoming a vet. Melanie had assumed that this was just a result of her cousin's problems in the first two Triple Crown races. But Christina sounded more conflicted now than she had before. "Either way you'd get to be around horses," Melanie pointed out.

"I know," Christina said. She had stuffed as many clothes as she could into Melanie's suitcase and was trying to zip it closed. "I just hate being so indecisive. I never thought I would be more confused *after* the Triple Crown than I was before it."

Melanie thought back to the spring. Before the Kentucky Derby, her focus had been solely on Image. Things had been simpler. Now she was torn between her responsibility to Image and her desire to become a professional jockey. "I don't have things figured out, either, Chris," Melanie said. "I'm not sure what my next step is supposed to be."

"You just want to get all the rides you can, right?"

"Yeah. But I'm starting to think that I should leave Kentucky and try to make it on my own, like Cindy did."

"I can't imagine Whitebrook without you," Christina said after a pause. "I know you would do great on your own, though."

"Where are you going to be?" Melanie was glad she and Christina had finally worked through their rivalry. Before the Kentucky Derby the chilly anger between them had made the Triple Crown tension worse, and Melanie had missed being able to confide in her cousin. Of all the people in the world, Christina was most capable of understanding what she was going through.

23

"I guess it mostly depends on Star and which trainers give me rides," Christina answered. "To be honest, I have no idea. Maybe I'll just take it a few weeks at a time."

A few weeks at a time. Melanie felt as though she needed to plan farther ahead than that. She had waited so long to become a full-time jockey, and now that she finally had the chance, she wanted to make the most of the coming summer.

LIKE ALL DREAMFLIGHT HORSES, NOBLE ANSWER WAS A bundle of nerves from the moment she stepped onto the track. Christina had to check the three-year-old filly multiple times as they circled the oval at an uneven jog. Nobie kept sticking her head up, trying to spit out the bit.

"I don't think we've found a bit that she likes yet," Aaron said as he rode up beside Christina on Callie, a dark bay Thoroughbred.

Christina smiled. She had become attached to Callie and his nervous spirit when she had been his jockey in the spring. Callie was a sprinter by training, but he had shown some promising staying power when the Johnstons entered him in distance races.

Christina wrestled Nobie's head back down with a

few quick pulls on the reins. "Doesn't the grinding sound drive you crazy?" The clicking of Nobie's teeth against the metal was making Christina clench her jaw.

Aaron shrugged. "I've gotten used to it. Sometimes she responds better to a few checks with the inside rein."

Christina tried what Aaron suggested, and the grinding stopped for several seconds. She relaxed her jaw and was about to thank Aaron when the grinding resumed. "Oh, well. The galloping will drown it out. How's Callie?"

"He's been great. I think he'll do well on Saturday as long as his leg doesn't give him any trouble."

"Have there been any signs that it's still bothering him?" Christina asked. She looked down at Callie's legs, unable to discern any hesitation in the colt's strides.

"Not really. Tendon injuries just make me nervous, since they can flare up again without warning." Aaron steadied Callie as the high-strung colt tried to kick out. "I need to let him canter before he explodes, but I want to hear all about Star's Triple Crown. Are you free for dinner tonight?"

Christina nodded. Evenings at Belmont had been quiet since Melanie had left. It would be nice to go into the city with a friend. "We can figure out a time and place later."

A few minutes after Aaron and Callie cantered away, Christina asked Nobie to switch gaits. The Johnstons wanted her to do a couple of warm-up laps at a jog and canter before clocking a half-mile breeze. They would do a longer breeze the next morning.

Christina felt a smile spread across her face as Nobie launched into a rocking canter. The filly's strong strides stirred up small clouds of dirt on the hard track. Whenever she rode in a morning workout Christina couldn't imagine anything she would rather be doing. What could be better than helping these young Thoroughbreds reach their potential as racers?

At moments like these Christina remembered the advice Vince Jones, the head trainer at Celtic Meadows in Kentucky, had given her. Vince had said that she should put off college and focus on racing while she was still young and strong. Maybe that wasn't such a bad idea.

When she had finished warming up Nobie, Christina turned to Patrick, waiting for his signal to start the breeze. Patrick dropped his arm just as Christina and Nobie passed the half-mile pole.

Christina crouched low over Nobie's neck and encouraged the filly forward with her legs and hands. The filly finally stopped mouthing the bit and lengthened her stride.

Even though all the horses at Dreamflight seemed overly skittish, Christina admired their ability to turn their nerves into power at a gallop. Nobie didn't have the blazing speed that Star and Callie did, but she ran gamely, covering the surface in long, fluid strides.

"Great ride," Patrick praised at the end of the

breeze. "You got her to settle nicely." He patted Nobie's nose. Now that she was no longer galloping, Nobie had resumed chewing the bit. "Why don't you ride Matt next?"

Christina looked over to the gap in the track, where a groom was holding Dreamflight's star, Matter of Time. The four-year-old had been the previous year's Horse of the Year. "When is he racing?"

"We've got him entered in the Suburban Handicap the weekend after next," Patrick replied. "It'll be a good starting point for his summer stakes campaign. Amanda and I figured you would be a great match for him." He held Nobie's head so that Christina could dismount. "You *are* still riding for us this summer, especially at Saratoga, right?"

"I wasn't sure you were serious about that," Christina said honestly. After she'd jockeyed Callie to victory in the San Felipe Stakes, the Johnstons had talked about making her their primary jockey at Saratoga. But they hadn't repeated the offer until now.

"Of course we were. Amanda's already factored you into our racing plans." Patrick began walking Nobie toward the gap.

Christina followed, biting her lip as she considered. When the Johnstons had originally asked her about Saratoga, she had hesitated because of Star. Back then the Triple Crown had been the only thing she could think about. But now that Star was getting a much-deserved break until the Travers Stakes, she was ready to explore her options as a jockey. The Johnstons' offer would be a great way to start.

Patrick handed Nobie's reins to Jessica, Dreamflight's head groom. "Congratulations on your Belmont win," Jessica said as she traded Matt for Nobie. "You'll have to tell me all about it later."

"No problem. You should join me and Aaron for dinner tonight," Christina offered.

Jessica looked away. "No, I think he wanted this to be an alone thing."

Christina tried to hide her surprise. When she had stayed at Dreamflight she and Aaron had become good friends. In April there had been signs that Aaron was interested in her. But they had barely kept in touch after she left California. Christina had assumed that Aaron was just asking her to dinner as a friend. Was he? "Well, maybe we can catch up later, Jessica," Christina said quickly. She let Patrick give her a leg up into Matt's saddle, momentarily pushing aside her questions about Aaron. Matt pranced sideways as she tried to get on, but Christina managed to swing her leg over the horse's back.

From the moment Matt set foot on the track, it was clear that he wanted to run. He high-stepped his way through the warm-up. His movements were jerky, and he kept lunging forward, trying to break into a dead run.

Christina kept checking the colt firmly, letting him know she would not tolerate such misbehavior. "You're not running until you settle down," she told

29

him, tapping him with her crop as he tried to skitter across the track.

Matt snorted and yanked on the reins. After several unsuccessful attempts to grab the bit, the colt finally settled into an even trot.

When they reached the clubhouse turn for the third time, Christina crouched forward, cueing the horse for a gallop. Within seconds she realized why Matt had been Horse of the Year. The horse accelerated with every stride, his hooves digging into the dirt and flinging it back. The grandstands and observers faded into a silvery blur as they rounded the turn, and the wind fanned out Matt's mane and tail.

"Attaboy!" Christina cried, almost laughing out loud in delight. This was what she loved most about racing. The best Thoroughbreds would run their hearts out when their riders gave them their heads. Matt was putting everything he had into this breeze.

Matt and Christina breezed halfway down the backstretch, flashing past the three-quarter pole, before Christina stood in the stirrups and brought Matt down to a canter. They cantered the rest of the way down the backstretch, rounding the far turn before slowing to a trot and then a walk. Christina sat back in the saddle, running a hand down Matt's neck. Matt's bay coat had barely darkened with sweat, and his breathing was only a little faster than normal.

"You're amazing, boy," Christina praised, rubbing

the horse's neck. "I can't wait to ride you in the Suburban."

When Christina brought Matt back to Patrick, the trainer was smiling. "Four furlongs in forty-six and three-fifths seconds," Patrick said, showing her the stopwatch. "Dreamflight could definitely use you this summer." He jotted a note on his clipboard. "Of course, you don't have to make that decision right away. Just let us know when you figure out your plans."

Christina gave Matt one last pat. "I've already made up my mind," she replied with a grin. "I'd love to ride for Dreamflight at Saratoga."

"Here's to the winner of the Belmont Stakes," Aaron said, raising his glass. "I hope you have many more victories this summer."

Christina clinked her glass against his. "And to you for getting your jockey's license. Here's to a great summer with Dreamflight's horses." Christina pulled back her glass and sipped at her raspberry Italian soda.

Aaron turned away from the table, sneezing twice. "Excuse me," he said, blowing his nose. "It's just my luck to come down with a cold now that summer's finally here. Maybe it has something to do with how little sleep I got last week because of finals."

Christina took a bite of her pasta. "Do you ever wish you didn't have to juggle classes and riding?"

"Sometimes," Aaron replied. "But I want to get my degree. I figure it will give me more options. My life would be so much easier if I was as sure about jockeying as you are."

Christina chuckled at the irony. It seemed amazing that she could give anyone the impression that she had everything figured out. "I'm not as sure as you think," she admitted. "I became a jockey because of Star, but he's only got another year or two of racing left in him. What happens then?"

"You'll find another amazing horse."

Christina wasn't so certain. She had bonded with Star from the very start, taking care of him when he'd been an orphaned foal. Her mother had shared a special bond with Star's dam, Ashleigh's Wonder, and even though Ashleigh had ridden hundreds of horses since her first victory on Wonder, Christina knew that her mother had not loved any of them as much.

"You were the one who told me there was nothing better than riding in a race," Aaron persisted.

"I still believe that," Christina said. She idly twirled some pasta around her fork. "But jockeying isn't just about the race. There's all the tension and politics, too."

"There's tension and politics in everything," Aaron pointed out.

"It's different with racing. Like last week, Alexis Huffman, the trainer for Speed.com, pretended that her horse was stolen. When Speed.com was found, the veterinary exam showed he had a fractured cannon bone. If he had raced in the Belmont, he would have broken down." Christina shuddered. "When I hear stories like that or think about what happened to Melanie in the Kentucky Derby, I wonder if being a jockey is the best way to help horses."

"But as a jockey, you're in the perfect position to help," Aaron argued. "Think about what Chris Antley did for Charismatic in the Belmont a few years ago."

Christina remembered watching that race on television. Charismatic had just crossed the finish line in third, losing his shot at the Triple Crown, when the colt's jockey jumped off the horse and called for help. X rays later showed that Charismatic had a lateral condylar fracture, the equine equivalent of a broken ankle. Chris Antley's quick reaction probably saved the horse from more serious injury.

"I know that I can do good things as a jockey," Christina replied. "I've just been rethinking my decision to delay college. Some people think I'm making a big mistake by not going to school right away. Others think that I'd be making a big mistake if I went to college instead of continuing with my jockeying career. It's hard to know whom to believe."

"Their opinions don't matter," Aaron said. "What's going to make you happiest?"

Christina laughed. "If I knew that, then all my stress would probably be over." She took another bite of pasta. "Thanks for listening, though. I could have used someone with your good sense over the past couple of months."

"I wish I could have been there." Aaron looked across the table at her, fixing her with his light brown eyes. "I was hoping we could go back to how close we were before the Santa Anita Derby," he added, a nervous tremor in his voice.

Christina looked down, stirring her soda with her straw to avoid Aaron's gaze. She had been slightly attracted to Aaron while she'd been in California. But that had been when she'd thought there was no hope for her and Parker. She and Aaron couldn't go back to how they had been in April, but Christina didn't want to hurt him. Aaron was one of the kindest people she had ever met.

Aaron seemed to read her expression. "Never mind, Christina. It was just an idle hope. I'm sorry."

"Don't apologize," Christina said. She stopped playing with her straw and forced herself to make eye contact. "I'll never forget what you did for me, Star, and Callie when I was at Dreamflight, Aaron. You were a great friend when I needed one."

"You said the same thing in April, but you implied things could be different between us after the Triple Crown."

Christina sighed, knowing that she owed Aaron the truth. "I just got back together with my ex-boyfriend."

"You told me that you were both too busy for a relationship."

"We still are, but we decided that we wanted to try to make things work." Christina knew it would be easier for her to date Aaron, whose schedule was more similar to hers. Yet as much as she enjoyed this friendship, her heart belonged to Parker. It had for the past two years. "I'm sorry if I—"

"You don't need to apologize, either," Aaron said, cutting her off. "Let's just pretend that the last few minutes of the conversation didn't happen, okay?" He waited for Christina's nod. "Now tell me more about what happened to Star during the Triple Crown."

The phone rang just as Christina was pulling on her boots for the workouts the next morning. She answered using the speakerphone function so that she could tie the laces as she spoke. "Hello?"

"Hi, Christina. It's Aaron." Aaron's voice sounded strange, distorted beyond the speakerphone static.

"Hi, Aaron. How are you?" Christina was surprised he was calling so soon. Their conversation at the end of dinner had been rather stilted, and she'd assumed that it would take some time for their friendship to recover from those awkward moments.

"I've been better." Aaron chuckled, as though the words were a joke, and then coughed away from the receiver.

"Is your cold still bothering you?" Christina asked with friendly concern.

"It flared up during the night," Aaron replied, sneezing. "I just went out to the track, but Amanda wouldn't let me ride." Aaron sneezed again.

"Considering how sick you sound, I don't blame her," Christina said. "You should get some rest."

Aaron blew his nose. "I don't think I have a choice. Actually, I was calling to see if you were interested in riding Callie in the Riva Ridge Breeders' Cup."

"You'll probably be better by then," Christina protested. Aaron had worked hard to become Callie's jockey. He deserved this ride. "Why don't we wait and see?"

"To be honest, Christina, I feel terrible right now," Aaron admitted. "I don't think I'll be a hundred percent by Saturday, and Callie deserves nothing less. You've done good things with him before." Aaron cleared his throat. His voice was getting hoarser by the minute. "After you ride him in his workout today, you'll remember all his funny habits."

Callie's high-strung nature made him difficult to control in a race. When Christina had been his jockey she worried that he would burn out well before the finish. But because of the colt's will to win, it was impossible not to enjoy riding him. "If you really want me to ride, I will. Feel free to change your mind if you start feeling better, though."

"Thanks, Christina," Aaron said with a sniffle.

"Take it easy, all right?" Christina finished lacing up her boots and looked at the clock. Ian was expecting her in five minutes. "I need to get to the track right now, but I have only one race this afternoon. Do you want me to bring you anything later?"

"I'll be okay." Aaron sneezed twice more, then groaned. "I should probably go back to bed. Good luck with Callie today."

"Thanks. I hope you feel better."

"Hey, boy. Remember me?" Christina asked Callie as Jessica led him onto the track.

Callie pawed the dirt.

"I think that's his way of saying yes," Jessica said. "Did Aaron talk to you this morning? He looked awful when he came by the track."

"He didn't sound very good when he called," Christina replied. "I was thinking of ordering some lunch for him. Would you mind bringing it over?" Christina figured that Aaron probably wasn't ready to see her.

"Sure," Jessica agreed. "Did something happen between the two of you yesterday?" She ducked her head, embarrassed. "You don't have to tell me if you don't want to. It's just that you two really hit it off back at Dreamflight. We all thought you were going to get together."

Christina patted Callie's nose. "Aaron's a great guy," she said carefully. "But I'm already dating someone else."

"Why didn't you tell Aaron about that earlier?" Jessica asked sharply.

"When I was in California Parker and I weren't dating," Christina said. She tried not to sound too defensive, reminding herself that Jessica was just trying to protect a friend. "Aaron and I only talked a few times after I left California. I didn't even know how he felt until last night. I didn't mean to hurt him, Jessica."

"I know," Jessica replied at last. "He's just such a nice person. I want him to be happy." There was an odd catch in Jessica's voice that made Christina wonder if the groom was interested in Aaron.

Christina took Callie's reins. "I should exercise this guy before he or the Johnstons get antsy," she said. "I'll find you later so we can decide what to get Aaron for lunch."

"Sounds good. Have a great ride."

"I'm sure we will." Christina patted Callie's neck. "Let's go, boy."

As usual, Callie was uncertain and anxious as he stepped onto the track. The colt arched his neck, snorting and darting sideways. When he was nervous Callie moved like a cat, his back end seemingly disconnected from his front end. Christina kept talking to him until he finally settled at the sound of her voice. By the time they completed the warm-up Callie had relaxed, allowing Christina to appreciate the power in his strides. The colt seemed to be more fit than he had been before his injury.

At the top of the stretch Christina crouched over Callie's withers and kneaded her fists along his neck. "Let's gallop!" she cried, giving him his head.

Callie shot forward, releasing all the energy he had been holding back. Just as she'd done when riding Matt the day before, Christina suppressed the urge to laugh out loud as the colt lengthened his stride and the wind whipped through his mane.

Callie's snorting breaths and the pounding of his hooves complemented the beating of Christina's heart as they flew through the three-furlong breeze. When they passed Patrick on the rail, Callie still had more to give. The colt protested Christina's renewed hold on the reins, wanting to keep running.

"You were awesome, boy," Christina praised when Callie finally slowed down. Back in California Callie had been a sweaty mess after every workout. But this time only traces of sweat dampened his neck and shoulders.

Christina looked up the track to where Patrick was waiting. Behind Patrick, Jessica was holding Nobie, and Anisa, another Dreamflight groom, was walking Matter of Time.

Christina smiled. She had already worked four horses for Whitebrook that morning, and now she had many more to exercise for Dreamflight. If she wanted, her riding schedule could be like this all summer. She couldn't wait.

4

MELANIE HADN'T THOUGHT IT WAS POSSIBLE FOR HER TO BE more nervous than she'd been before the Kentucky Derby. But as she reached for Image's halter her hands were shaking harder than they ever had.

"It's going to be okay, Mel," Jazz said, massaging her shoulders. "Image is ready."

"But one bolt could undo everything," Melanie replied, shrugging Jazz's hands off. They were going to try walking the filly on soft ground that morning. After countless hours in the Townsend Acres therapy pool, Image was finally ready for more conventional rehabilitation.

"We tranquilized her. She'll be all right," Jazz reassured her.

Melanie didn't want to rely on tranquilizers for

Image, but the filly was too unpredictable and fragile to be walked without them. "I can't help being scared."

"I know, but you have to calm down or else Image will pick up on your emotions."

Melanie nodded, taking deep breaths. She held Jazz's hand, squeezing it tightly. "I'm all right," she said in between breaths. "Let's walk her." When she reached for Image's emerald-colored halter again, her hands were steady.

Image stepped outside her huge, airy stall with some hesitation. The filly nudged Melanie's shoulder and whinnied nervously.

"Easy, girl. We're just going outside for a while." Melanie ran a reassuring hand along Image's neck. She looked down at Image's left leg, remembering the unnatural bend in it when the filly had gone down after the Kentucky Derby. The surgeons had been able to repair the cannon bone fracture by inserting implants that could support a thousand pounds of force. Melanie hoped fervently that the strength of the implants would not be tested that day.

When she walked out of her stall Image immediately turned in the direction of the therapy pool. Melanie gently tugged on the lead, maneuvering Image toward a patch of soft grass. "Not now, sweetie. We'll let you swim later." Image spent a couple of hours in the pool each day. Swimming was the only exercise that wouldn't exert force on her injured leg.

As Image followed Jazz and Melanie around the

patch of grass, Melanie glanced at the Townsend Acres medical facility. When she had first seen these buildings, she had been amazed at the state-of-the-art technology. The farm had its own attending veterinarian, surgery center, and rehabilitation facilities. Melanie had never imagined that her horse would put so many of these resources to use.

James Dalton, the Townsend Acres vet, was walking a horse into one of the other stalls. He waved to Melanie and Jazz as they walked past, and Melanie waved back. Dr. Dalton's expert care had been critical to Image's recovery.

"Have you talked to Dr. Dalton about moving Image yet?" Melanie asked. She put some slack in the lead rope, not wanting the filly to sense her tension. However, she made sure her hands were in a position where she could tighten her grip easily if Image started to skitter.

Jazz shook his head. "I wanted to see how she did today first."

"Are you still worried about paying for the care?" Melanie made a slow circle. Image followed obediently.

"Image is worth whatever Brad asks me to pay."

"You didn't answer my question," Melanie said. She patted Image's neck. The filly's ears flicked back at the touch.

"Let's not talk about this now." Jazz also stroked

Image's neck. "We have more important things to worry about."

Melanie started to protest, but she didn't want her tone to upset Image. Instead she walked the filly in silence, occasionally looking over at Jazz. Jazz's dark hair was pulled back in a ponytail, and he was wearing his usual low-slung jeans and baggy shirt. He would dress up for the Pegasus concert the next day, but Melanie thought he was more handsome like this. Then again, the longer she worked with horses, the less attention she paid to her own appearance. When she had first come to Whitebrook at age twelve, Melanie had made fun of the way Christina dressed. Now she and her cousin both dressed the same way.

Jazz checked his watch. "We should take her back. We only wanted to be out for five minutes, right?"

Melanie nodded. They were keeping this first session short. "You did great, girl," Melanie said to Image. She rubbed the filly's nose. Image's head was drooping a little from the tranquilizers, but her soft brown eyes were still bright. Looking into Image's eyes, Melanie could easily remember why she'd fallen in love with the filly in the first place.

"She's still a champion," Jazz said.

Image raised her head, nickering her agreement.

After they settled Image in her stall, Jazz and Melanie went back to the cottage for lunch. The yellow guest cottage stood at one edge of the Townsend Acres property, and it had obviously been designed for important guests. On the outside, tall oak trees shaded a small paddock. The security cameras around the paddock had been used to guard Image before the Kentucky Derby. Inside the cottage, the kitchen had every possible appliance, the den contained a large television and entertainment center, and the bedroom had a king-size bed with a wrought-iron frame.

Melanie would have traded all these comforts for the ability to take Image back to Whitebrook, where the filly belonged.

"Do you want your usual turkey and Swiss cheese?" Jazz asked as he toasted some bread.

Melanie nodded as she pulled packages of deli meats and cheeses out of the refrigerator. Not being enough of a cook to take advantage of all these modern appliances, she usually prepared simple meals. "And you want ham and cheese with mayonnaise, right?"

Jazz put the toast onto plates. "Our lives may be unpredictable, but at least our food isn't," he said. As he reached for the meat he added, "Actually, I was thinking that my life has been way too quiet without racing."

"You'll have Image's foals to keep you busy in a few years." As Melanie spoke she wondered whether those words were true. If Brad had things his way, he would breed Image to Celtic Mist and keep that foal as payment for Image's rehabilitation.

"But what about now?" Jazz spread some mayonnaise on the bread. "Once I pay off the vet bills for Image, I think I'm going to start looking for another racehorse. Want to be partners again?"

Partners. Jazz had used that word to describe their relationship when he had become Image's full owner. Image had finished second in the Florida Derby that day, beating colts for the first time. After that race, speculation about whether Image would run in the Kentucky Derby had been rampant, and when Melanie and Jazz had finally announced their plans for the Triple Crown, the media circus had descended upon Image. Through all this, Jazz had offered help and support. He had buoyed Melanie's spirits when she had worried about Image's ability to run a good race, and he had been her confidant when it seemed as though everyone else at Whitebrook was mad at her for pitting Image against Star.

As she remembered about all the good moments with Image, Melanie knew it would be easy for her to agree. But was she ready to dedicate herself to a new horse after the end of Image's racing career? And even if she was, did her plan to become a top jockey leave her with enough time to train another racehorse?

"What's wrong, Mel? Was I too overbearing with Image?" Jazz asked teasingly.

Melanie shook her head. She stopped making her sandwich, suddenly losing her appetite. "That's not it at all. I'm just not sure I can devote as much time to another horse as I devoted to Image." She didn't tell

Jazz about her fears that another horse she worked with could be injured as badly as Image had been. After all, if he had gotten over these worries, then so could she.

"Why not? Wasn't Image worth it?" Jazz's voice rose.

"Of course she was!" Melanie snapped, angry that Jazz could even ask that question. She swallowed back more angry remarks, trying to stay logical. "I want to be a jockey, Jazz. Jockeys have to move from track to track all year. I can't stay in Kentucky or spend too much time training any one horse."

Jazz remained silent. His jaw jutted out in a pout, and his eyes betrayed how hurt he was.

"You couldn't have become a star musician if you hadn't taken your band away from home," Melanie reasoned. "Come on, Jazz. I'm not saying no. I just want some time to think about it."

Jazz nodded tightly. His hands, which had been clenched, relaxed. "You're right," he said, sitting down to eat. "I just enjoyed working together so much that it's hard to think we won't be able to do it again." Jazz held up his hand to stop Melanie from interrupting him. "You don't have to explain, Mel. We can talk about it later."

The next evening Melanie hurried downstairs at the insistent ringing of the cottage doorbell. She looked through the peephole and saw Katie, Charlene, Barbara, and Dominique waiting on the doorstep.

"Hey, you're early," she greeted, letting them in. Jazz had given Melanie five front-row tickets to the concert.

"Of course we are. It's a Pegasus concert!" Charlene replied, almost squealing.

Melanie smiled. It was hard for her to see the members of Jazz's band as celebrities. Then again, she hadn't been very interested in music until she had started dating Jazz. She looked into the walk-in closet, trying to find the black boots to match her black halter top and leopard-print skirt. "I'll be ready in a sec. What have you been up to this summer?"

"I'm doing some work with the local theater. We're putting on *Annie* in July," Katie replied. Katie had held lead roles in both school musicals that year, and she planned to continue studying drama at the University of Kentucky that fall. "That should keep me busy until our road trip."

Melanie vaguely remembered hearing about her friends' plans to drive from Kentucky to California, where Barbara and Dominique were going to college. She and Christina had been invited, but both of them had commitments on the track. "It's too bad New York isn't on the way. You could stop by and watch Christina and me ride. Instead you'll just have to send us postcards." She pulled on her boots and grabbed her keys. "Okay, I'm ready. Let's go."

47

Dominique had brought along a Pegasus CD, and they listened to it on the drive. The girls knew all the words to the band's hit song, "Make My Day," and they had heard the CD enough to sing along with most of the other songs.

Barbara cranked up the volume before "Secret Destiny," the seventh track on the album. "The bassist has a great solo in this one," she said. She looked over at Melanie. "I know the lead singer's taken, but I can still go for the bassist, right?"

Melanie laughed, nodding. "I don't think Lyle has a girlfriend right now. He's kind of a goofball, though."

"What about the keyboardist?" Dominique asked.

"I think Arnold's single. Nuke's the only one who's married." When Image had raced in the Florida Derby in March, Melanie had met Nuke's wife, Kristi.

"Are they going to play any new songs tonight?" Charlene wondered. "You said they were working on new material. What does it sound like?"

"Jazz hasn't played any of it for me yet."

"But you see him all the time," Katie said as she hummed along to the song's chorus.

"We've been too busy with Image to talk about music." That morning's session had also gone smoothly, even with the tension between Jazz and Melanie. Melanie was still thinking about Jazz's offer. Maybe she would have some time to consider it. After all, Jazz had to pay Image's medical bills first. Melanie shook her head. She wasn't going to think about any of it that night.

48

Dominique laughed. "Sometimes I don't think you notice anything that doesn't have four legs, Mel."

Melanie stuck her tongue out. "If you promise to be nicer to me, then I'll let you in on a secret about Pegasus's newest song," she said in a conspiratorial whisper. All her friends stopped talking, and Barbara turned down the volume on the stereo. "Apparently it's going to be a ballad called 'Long Shot.'"

The Jazz Taylor onstage seemed different from the Jazz Taylor who helped Melanie clean Image's stall and bathe the filly after races. While performing, Jazz had to be glibly charming. He was a real crowd pleaser, making jokes and tossing guitar picks and small autographed posters into the audience.

Pegasus's performance was amazing. They had the entire amphitheater of screaming fans, mostly girls, on their feet. When the band played "Make My Day," Jazz aimed the microphone toward the crowd, letting them sing the chorus. The noise was so deafening that Melanie could barely hear the words Jazz did sing.

The band left the stage after "Make My Day" but came back when the crowd demanded an encore. Jazz took the microphone, walking closer to the crowd. The cameras followed his movements, projecting his picture onto the huge screens on either side of the stage. "As many of you know, I am the proud owner of a three-year-old filly named Perfect Image. Last month

Image proved that she was among the fastest horses in the world, and I wrote this song in honor of her Kentucky Derby victory."

As Nuke began providing the backbeat, Jazz jumped down from the stage, walking toward Melanie. Jazz reached out his hand, taking Melanie's and giving it a tight squeeze. "Melanie Graham, this song is dedicated to you." He raised her hand to his lips, kissing it.

Beside Melanie, Barbara and Charlene were squealing and jumping up and down. Jazz smiled at them as he took the stage again and began singing.

Melanie strained her ears, wanting to hear every word of Jazz's new song. The cheers from the crowd drowned out parts of the verses, but the words from the chorus stuck in her mind.

They told me never to bet on long shots, but never is a long time. Sometimes you have to take a chance and let a long shot steal your heart.

Melanie swayed in time to the soft rhythm as Jazz repeated those lines. She could not take her eyes away from his face. He was grinning broadly as he walked along the stage, drawing the crowd into his performance. It was like he belonged on the stage. Melanie wondered if Jazz loved performing as much as she loved jockeying.

Sometimes you have to take a chance and let a long shot steal your heart. . . .

Jazz held the last note, casting a spell over the crowd. In the moments of silence before the enthusiastic applause, Jazz again looked toward Melanie and winked at her.

Melanie winked back, and when the cheering resumed, she tried to yell the loudest.

5

CHRISTINA ALWAYS HAD TROUBLE EATING BEFORE A BIG race. With all the adrenaline racing through her, she usually just choked down a quick breakfast after the morning workouts. But on Saturday morning Callie's owner, Marisa Pavlik, invited her and the Johnstons to have brunch at Belmont's elegant Garden Terrace Dining Room.

While the others helped themselves to pancakes, scrambled eggs, and sausage, Christina picked at her fruit salad. She tried to insert an occasional word into the polite conversation as she rearranged the melon, pineapple, and orange slices on her plate.

Marisa was an entertainment journalist. The previous week she had gone to the premieres for several big movies, standing on the red carpet and asking the stars what they thought would be a good name for a racehorse. "Some of the responses were unmentionably inappropriate," Marisa told them in a confiding whisper. "There were a few good ideas, though. It's something for me to keep in mind when I breed Callie. Of course, I hope he has a few more good races left in him before he retires."

"He does," Patrick assured her. "He's been training like a champ for this race, and you know he'll run his best for Christina."

Christina felt her cheeks redden as she took another bite of cantaloupe, chewing slowly. She tried to forget that she was riding in two graded stakes races that afternoon and that her performance in these races would influence the number of rides the Johnstons offered her for the rest of the summer.

"He did last time," Marisa agreed. "If he wins this race, what's next?"

"Well, there's the Dwyer Stakes at the beginning of July. It's a mile and a sixteenth, just like the San Felipe," Amanda replied. "Depending on how Callie does there, we can try some of the big Saratoga stakes races. I was thinking about the Jim Dandy in early August."

"What about the fall? Should I be thinking about paying a supplemental nomination fee for the Breeders' Cup?" Marisa asked.

"We should probably wait a while before discussing that," Patrick said. "If he keeps running like he did before his injury, though, then he should have enough points to qualify."

Christina knew better than to look too far ahead, but she couldn't help getting excited at the mention of the Breeders' Cup. She hoped the Johnstons would stay with shorter races for Callie, giving him an opportunity to win the Breeders' Cup Sprint. With luck, she and Star would be running in the Classic that day, too.

After brunch Christina went to visit Callie. Callie had his head hanging over the stall door, and he nickered as she approached.

"Hey, gorgeous," Christina greeted him, rubbing Callie's face and combing her fingers through his forelock. Callie nudged her affectionately, and Christina rested her head against his neck. His clipped redbrown coat tickled her face. "You're going to run fast for me today, right?"

"He'll certainly try," a teasing voice replied.

Christina turned to see Aaron behind her. He was carrying a grooming box. "Hey, Aaron. How are you feeling?" she asked. This was the first time she'd seen him since they'd had dinner on Wednesday.

"Much better," Aaron answered. His voice still sounded a little raw. "I think this was just my body's way of forcing me to sleep for a couple of days. By the way, did Jessica give you my thanks for the food?"

"Yes. You're welcome." Christina wondered whether she was right about Jessica being interested in Aaron. If she was, could Aaron, in turn, become interested in Jessica? Christina had seen the playful interactions between them at Dreamflight, and she thought they could make each other happy.

Aaron grabbed Callie's halter and let himself into the stall. "Shouldn't you be in the jockeys' lounge?"

"I'm going to change in a few minutes," Christina said. She gestured to the duffel bag on the floor. It contained Dreamflight's hunter-green-and-white diamond-patterned racing silks. "I just wanted to see the horses first." She gave Callie one last pat. "For the record, I still think you should be riding this silly horse today."

Aaron reached into his pocket for a tissue to blow his nose. "I somehow doubt Callie would give me much sympathy even if he knew I was sick," he joked. "I know you'll do great with him."

There was a long pause as both Christina and Aaron searched for something else to say. Aaron spoke first. "Listen, Christina, about Wednesday—"

"Like you said, we shouldn't let that conversation get in the way of our friendship, okay?" Christina smiled tentatively.

Aaron nodded, returning the smile. "I'll see you after the races."

• • •

55

"The horses are loading for the two-hundred-thousand-dollar Riva Ridge Breeders' Cup." Christina could barely hear the announcer's voice as she and Callie waited for their turn to load. Callie had never been a big fan of starting gates, so she wanted to keep him as quiet as possible until the final moments. "The race will be seven furlongs. The record time of one minute twenty and one-fifth seconds was set by You and I in 1994."

Sometimes Christina had to suppress an urge to laugh when she heard the record time for a given race. Most big Thoroughbred races were over in less than two minutes. This sprint had been done in eighty seconds. How could time slow down so much for the jockeys during a race?

To calm herself as the horses continued to load, Christina began reciting the instructions the Johnstons had given her in the walking ring. The trainers had been in a good mood because she had guided Nobie to a second-place finish in the Vagrancy Handicap earlier that afternoon. "You're breaking from the outside, so just get him to the rail as soon as you can," Amanda had instructed. "It's a short race, so he should have no problem leading wire to wire."

The trainer's voice echoed in Christina's mind until the attendants finally called Callie's number. They were breaking from the seventh post position in an eight-horse race. Callie started backing up as the attendants approached. Christina tightened her legs around his sides, sitting through his catlike shying motions. She could feel his quivering muscles beneath her. Looking down, Christina saw that sweat was already darkening his bay coat.

"You're all right, Callie," Christina murmured, rubbing the base of the colt's neck. She applied more pressure with her legs, and the colt took a few hesitant steps forward.

Callie protested again when he entered the gate, lashing out in the claustrophobically small area. But the attendants managed to slam the gate shut behind him, and Christina soothed him with her voice and hands.

"Let's win this," she whispered as the gate crew yelled that they were loading the last horse. Christina grabbed a chunk of Callie's long black mane to prepare for the leaping start. She took a deep breath, exhaling just as the starting bell rang and the gates flew open.

Callie broke cleanly, already pushing forward and fighting for the bit. Christina immediately edged him toward the inner railing, needing to save ground in the short race. Because the horses that had drawn inside post positions had also broken well, she had to settle Callie behind them.

Christina concentrated on finding an opening, trying to tune out the thundering hooves, the loud, snorting breaths of the racehorses, and the roar of the crowd. Above all this, the announcer's voice rang from the loudspeakers. "Windsong takes the early lead! Congress of Vienna and Star Scroll are neck and neck at the rail, followed by Calm Before the Storm and Sunrise Sonata."

Ahead of her, Christina could see the horses fighting for the lead. She looked to her outside and saw a small gap between Star Scroll and Congress of Vienna. Before she and Callie could shoot through it, Congress of Vienna drifted in, blocking them.

Christina felt Callie tensing beneath her. The colt's gait was choppy even when he was calm, but when Callie was frustrated, the up-and-down motion became jolting. Christina grabbed another handful of mane, trying to keep her balance. She forced back growing feelings of panic. She and Star had come in last in the Kentucky Derby because they had been boxed in. She couldn't let that happen again.

Christina looked to her left. Windsong was dropping back, leaving a small gap along the rail. She hauled on her inside rein. Callie lunged toward the rail.

"As they come around the far turn, Congress of Vienna takes the lead, but Star Scroll is in hot pursuit. Windsong appears to be out of it, but Calm Before the Storm has found some room along the rail. The Dreamflight colt moves up to fourth. . . ."

Christina kneaded her hands along Callie's neck and tapped him a couple of times with her crop, encouraging him to move. The colt stretched his head forward, lengthening his stride as he clicked into a higher gear. "Come on, Callie!" she yelled, barely hearing her own words. The colt passed Windsong, but the other two horses were more than a length ahead and showing no signs of tiring.

Christina kept herself still in the saddle now, knowing that Callie was giving everything he had. The pounding of his strides accelerated as he powered toward the leaders.

One-two-three. One-two-three. One-two-three. One—

Suddenly Christina lurched in the saddle. Callie had taken a misstep, breaking the smooth, quickening rhythm. The next galloping beats were jolting, making Christina's teeth clatter together.

Instinctively Christina pulled back on the reins, wanting to be sure that Callie was not hurt. Callie shook his head, fighting the restraint.

"Whoa, boy. Let's slow down, okay?" Christina gave the reins another tug.

Callie ignored Christina. He continued running with rough but strong strides, accelerating until he was almost even with the other horses.

Christina tried to check Callie's strides for lameness, but the colt's agitation was adding to the unevenness of his gait. She couldn't tell what was the cause of this rough gallop. Christina started to pull back on the reins again, but the continuing strength of Callie's strides made her hesitate. Was she willing to ruin Callie's chances of winning this race when she couldn't be sure that he was hurt?

Christina adjusted her grip on the reins, considering. So many people were counting on her to win this race. Marisa and the Johnstons expected Callie to do well. They were already planning his future. If she stopped him when nothing was wrong, she would disappoint everyone.

With the finish line approaching quickly, Callie passed Star Scroll. But Congress of Vienna was still half a length ahead. Refusing to concede defeat, Callie dug in deeper. The colt stumbled again as he tried to find another gear.

This time Christina did not hesitate. She stood in her stirrups and hauled back on the reins. Even so, Callie would not stop. He hobbled across the finish line on three legs, still trying to catch Congress of Vienna.

Heedless of the danger, Christina threw herself out of the saddle. She clutched Callie's reins in her right hand, still trying to slow the colt. Callie ignored her signals, lunging forward. He dragged Christina along with him, sending a bolt of pain through her right wrist.

"I need some help here!" Christina yelled, trying to keep her balance. The world was swimming before her eyes, making it hard for her to see. She tugged on the reins again, crying out at her wrist's sharp protest. Callie jerked his head and whirled toward her, his breathing shallow and rapid. He nickered in panic as other horses swerved around him.

Christina was finally able to take the reins in both hands. Bracing herself, she pulled back in a series of sharp jerks. The pain in her wrist seemed more distant now, a detached sort of throbbing. Callie whirled around, trying to challenge the remaining horses. "Whoa, boy. You ran a good race. But you have to listen to me now, Callie. You have to stop." Panic made Christina's words run together. She had to get Callie under control.

Callie hobbled from side to side, holding his right foreleg off the ground. As Christina struggled to keep her hold on the reins, she could see the whites of the horse's eyes. "You're going to be all right, boy," she said, repeating the words like a litany. "Everything's going to be okay."

At last Christina heard the two-toned siren of the equine ambulance. Two track vets Christina recognized, Drs. Murphy and Stucker, rushed onto the scene. They startled Callie, who began backing away from them.

"We need to tranquilize him," Dr. Stucker said. He reached for an injection kit. "If he puts too much weight on that leg . . ."

Christina was certain that she didn't want to hear the end of that sentence. Again she tugged on Callie's reins, still trying to get him to stand. The colt swung his hindquarters around, eyeing the vets suspiciously. When Dr. Stucker approached with a needle, Callie squealed and reared, lashing out with his front legs.

Christina tumbled to the ground as Callie jerked the reins from her grasp.

The world seemed to move in slow motion as Callie landed heavily on his front legs. His right leg buckled with a sickening crunch, and Callie went down painfully on his right side.

Christina cried out. She leaped to her feet and hurried over to the colt. Dr. Stucker was administering the tranquilizer, and this time Callie didn't seem to notice the needle. The bay horse was in shock. Christina ran her uninjured hand down Callie's trembling form. The sweat from his coat soaked through her riding gloves. "The vets are here now, Callie," Christina whispered, feeling his heaving sides. She wasn't sure Callie could hear her anymore. His ears were flicking frantically, and his eyes were so wide that they seemed completely white. "They're going to make it better. They have to." Christina continued to run her hands down Callie's sides, wanting to offer what little comfort she could.

"What's wrong?" Patrick's voice broke through the vets' terse instructions to each other. Christina hadn't realized the trainer had arrived.

Dr. Murphy didn't look up as he applied a temporary cast to the injury. "He shattered his sesamoids and tore multiple ligaments in his ankle."

Christina gasped at the severity of the injury. She broke out in a cold sweat and bent over Callie's neck, certain that she was going to throw up.

Patrick tapped her on the shoulder. "Let's give the vets some room to work, Christina."

Christina swallowed back the bitter bile in her throat. "We can't leave Callie alone," she said frantically. "He'll panic if we're not here."

"They're taking him to the hospital," Patrick told her softly. "I'm going to ride with him, and Aaron will follow in a car. You can go with him." Patrick gently helped her to her feet. "Don't worry about the race, Christina. You did the best you could."

Christina stared at Patrick, unable to reply. Any halfway decent jockey would have pulled the colt up after the first stumble. Christina felt her knees start to shake.

Someone else pulled her away and made her sit down. Christina barely recognized the sound of Aaron's voice when he began speaking. "Put your head between your knees," he instructed. "Take a deep breath."

Christina couldn't stem her hysteria. She looked toward the accident scene. Her vision wavered and blurred as she watched the vets load Callie into the ambulance.

"Please be careful with him!" she yelled, her voice cracking. "You have to save him. Please save him!"

6

"ARE YOU READY TO HEAD OUT?" CINDY ASKED.

Melanie checked the girth on Rush Street, the big bay three-year-old that she would be riding on the trails, and tightened it a notch. "Yeah. Let's go." She stifled a yawn. She had stayed up late after Jazz's concert but still gotten up at five to exercise horses for Townsend Acres. Exercise riding was one of the many ways she was trying to repay Brad for what he had done for Image. Despite her exhaustion, Melanie had not wanted to cancel this trail ride with Cindy. She needed the older woman's advice.

Cindy led Dove, a small gray Arabian mare, to the mounting block. Blond-haired Cindy had been a champion jockey for over fifteen years before shoulder surgery had forced her to change careers. Although she could no longer ride the high-strung Thorough-breds, Cindy still had a deep understanding of how to make them run. As Tall Oaks' head trainer, she had guided an unpredictable racehorse named Gratis to solid placings in the Kentucky Derby and the Belmont. Gratis had also crossed the finish line third in the Preakness, but illegal riding by his jockey had led to a disqualification.

"Take it easy with Rush Street today," Cindy instructed. "I don't want to put too much stress on his legs before we ship him to Belmont."

As a two-year-old, Rush Street had been an early favorite for the Triple Crown races. The colt had come in second in the Breeders' Cup Juvenile. But a suspensory ligament tear had kept him from training for most of the winter and spring. He had only recently begun racing again, winning a stakes race at Churchill Downs. Cindy had entered the colt in the Suburban Handicap, wanting to see if he could regain his old form.

"I will," Melanie replied, asking Rush Street to walk beside Dove.

"So what did you want to talk about?" Cindy asked as they walked along the wooded trail. "Is something wrong?"

Melanie shook her head. "I just wanted to know more about what it was like for you at the beginning of your career. You started out at Belmont when you were eighteen, right?"

"Yeah. I went there after my trip to Dubai," Cindy answered. "The first years were hard. I was determined to prove that I could be a great jockey without using Whitebrook's name, so I started out at the bottom, grooming and riding claimers. I got a few lucky breaks, but it was a pretty lonely life."

Rush Street tried to break into a trot. Melanie checked him lightly, holding him back. "I'm thinking about going out on my own like you did."

"Are you sure, Mel?" Cindy asked. "Like I said, I was lonely. The first couple of years I realized how much I still had to learn about the racing world. It made me wish that I had stayed around Whitebrook longer."

"How am I going to get other trainers to notice me if I don't break away from Whitebrook and establish myself independently?"

"You'll get enough notice if you keep riding as well as you are now," Cindy replied. She cued Dove into a slow jog and motioned for Melanie to do the same with her mount. "I mean, you've already got a Kentucky Derby win under your belt. I wish I'd had the chance to win that race." Cindy sighed.

"But you won the Dubai World Cup when you were sixteen." Melanie had watched that race on tape many times, marveling at the power of Wonder's Champion, who was a half brother to Star.

A small smile crossed Cindy's lips. "I never talked much about that race, especially after Champion was sent to Dubai. Sometimes I can hardly believe he's back in Kentucky."

Mike and Ashleigh had sold Wonder's Champion to Ben al-Rihani's father over ten years before. Melanie didn't know much about the sale, since it was never discussed at Whitebrook. All she knew was that when Ben became the owner of Tall Oaks, he had brought Champion back to Kentucky for Cindy. "Champion looks a lot like Star," Melanie said. Both horses resembled their dam, Ashleigh's Wonder, who had died shortly after Star's birth.

"He had more of Gratis's personality, though," Cindy said. "Champion was impossible as a two-year-old. He spent most of his time trying to outsmart his rider."

"Sounds like Image," Melanie said.

"How is she doing?"

"Better. Jazz is going to ask Dr. Seymour to give us a second opinion." Dr. Seymour was Whitebrook's vet.

"Are you thinking about moving her before Brad gives you too much trouble?" Cindy asked.

"I don't know." Melanie sighed. She guessed that Cindy had heard that Brad wanted Image's first foal as payment. "I know Brad can't be trusted, but Image is more important. I have to do whatever it takes to make sure she's going to be all right."

"How much longer are you going to work with her before you go back to Belmont?" Cindy slowed her horse as they came to a stream.

67

"Probably another week or so. I want to start riding in more races now that school isn't in the way." Melanie had stayed in touch with the Johnstons since leaving Belmont, and she hoped they would offer her more mounts. She envied Christina, who was riding for the famous West Coast trainers in two stakes races that afternoon.

"Well, if you're going to be at Belmont next week, how would you like to ride Rush Street in the Suburban?"

"Do you even have to ask?" Melanie gave Cindy a grateful smile. "I'd love to."

Cindy nodded. "I'll tell Ben." She paused before adding, "I know you don't want to hear this, Mel, but I don't think you should give up on school so quickly."

Melanie tried not to roll her eyes. "You aren't the first person who's told me that." All her relatives had encouraged her to reconsider this choice.

"I didn't think college was important when I was eighteen, either," Cindy said. "Looking back, I think that maybe I should have spent a few more years taking classes and riding with Whitebrook."

"If you had stayed at Whitebrook, then you might not have gotten all those amazing opportunities in New York," Melanie argued.

"Maybe not," Cindy agreed. "But there probably would have been others. By leaving Whitebrook so early, I missed out on the chance to ride Honor Bright in some of her biggest races."

Honor Bright was a broodmare at Whitebrook. She had won the Breeders' Cup Distaff as a four-year-old. "At least you got to ride her daughter in the Kentucky Derby," Melanie pointed out. Honor and Glory had placed third in that race seven years earlier.

Cindy smiled. "Honor and Glory was amazing. She would have run for anyone. I should visit her after dinner tonight. Maybe I'll bring some carrots for her dam and sire, too."

Ashleigh and Mike had invited some family friends over for dinner. Melanie was still trying to figure out what to bring. "I'm sure Glory will be glad to see you," she said. Cindy had played a large role in March to Glory's training. The horse had set a record in the Breeders' Cup Classic and had been named Horse of the Year after his three-year-old season.

"I missed him during all those years that I was at Belmont," Cindy said. "And I know you would miss Image and some of the other Whitebrook horses if you went out on your own." When Melanie remained silent, Cindy added, "I'm not saying that you shouldn't try to get rides with other trainers. In fact, I think that's a great idea. I just don't want you to make the same mistake I did. I left Whitebrook because I thought the only way to be successful was to prove to the racing world that I didn't need the people who had taught me so much. It took me a long time to realize that the only person I had to prove anything to was myself. Please don't do the same thing."

Melanie nodded. "I'll think about what you said," she promised. Beneath her, Rush Street kicked out restlessly, frustrated by the easy pace.

"He's telling us that we should stop talking and let him stretch his legs," Cindy said. She cued Dove into a slow canter. "I think he's right." Looking over her shoulder, Cindy asked, "Are you coming?"

Smiling, Melanie asked Rush Street to follow.

As Melanie parked her car in the driveway in front of her aunt and uncle's house, she tried to figure out how long it had been since she had spent more than a couple of hours at Whitebrook. Despite all the luxuries of Townsend Acres, she missed Whitebrook's friendlier, more relaxed atmosphere.

On her way to the farm Melanie had stopped by the store to pick up a couple of bottles of sparkling apple cider. She figured her turkey-and-cheese sandwiches would have been out of place next to the specialties that Beth McLean, Ian's wife, usually prepared.

When Melanie entered the Reeses' living room, the first thing she noticed was the volume of the television. Kevin McLean, one of her classmates, was sitting inches away from the screen. His eyes were glued to the World Cup soccer match. Kevin had been a star soccer player in high school and would be attending Kentucky State on a soccer scholarship in the fall.

"Hey, Mel. Long time no see," Kevin greeted her,

barely taking his eyes off the game. "How's Image?" Kevin had been a big help during Image's early training.

"She's doing better. We walked her on soft ground for ten minutes today," Melanie replied. She walked closer to the television to check the score. "Who else is coming?"

"Samantha and Tor are on their way, but Cindy and Ben just called to say that they're going to be late." Samantha was Kevin's older sister. She and her husband, Tor, owned Whisperwood Farm, a training facility for jumpers, eventers, and steeplechasers. Until Parker had gotten a grant with the United States Equestrian Team, he and his horse, Foxglove, had trained there.

Melanie took her cider bottles into the kitchen. "I brought some drinks," she told Beth and Ashleigh. "It's mainly for Kevin and me, but I figured Samantha might want some, too." Samantha had recently announced that she was going to have a baby.

"I'm sure she will," Ashleigh said, checking the food in the oven. "Why don't you pry Kevin from the soccer game and make him set the table?"

Kevin didn't respond to this request until Melanie finally picked up the remote control and turned off the game. "You'll be playing so much soccer soon that you'll get sick of it," she said when Kevin began to sulk.

"I'll get sick of soccer when you get sick of riding," Kevin replied teasingly.

As usual, the dinner conversation centered on horses. Ashleigh and Mike talked about what was happening at Belmont. Melanie suppressed a pang of jealousy at the thought of Christina riding all of Whitebrook's young prospects. If she had stayed at the track, then she would have shared in these opportunities.

Samantha and Tor also joined in the conversation, mentioning their new breeding program and discussing how much help Parker was giving them.

"I know he must miss his horses, though," Samantha said. Parker's horses, Foxglove and Wizard of Oz, were still in England. "He calls every day to check on them. I know he'll be happy to get back to England, but we're going to miss him. I don't know how anything's going to get done around Whisperwood, since my husband seems to believe I'm too fragile to work more than a few hours a day."

"There's nothing wrong with being careful," Tor said. He looked over at Melanie. "Has Parker stopped by your cottage since you got back?"

Melanie shook her head. "But I haven't been there much lately."

"I was just asking because I think Parker's avoiding Townsend Acres," Tor explained. "He and his father are fighting about whether he should go back to England."

Parker and his father had been feuding for as long as Melanie could remember. "Parker's grant pays for his training in England. He doesn't need Brad's permission, does he?"

"No, but Brad can make his life difficult," Samantha replied. "We probably shouldn't be talking about this behind Parker's back, though."

"Cindy told me that she went on a trail ride with you this morning, Melanie," Beth said, changing the subject. "Who did you ride?"

"Rush Street," Melanie answered. "Cindy wants me to be his jockey for the Suburban." She paused, momentarily debating whether to share the conclusions she had come to at the end of the trail ride. "I think that I'm going to stay at Belmont after the Suburban and then go straight to Saratoga. I want to go out on my own and start getting rides with other trainers."

"What about Image?" Ashleigh asked.

"Image is doing a lot better. There are at least half a dozen people at Townsend Acres who can do what I do with her now," Melanie said. "If there were any big summer meets in Kentucky, then I would stay with her. But I have to start riding in New York if I want to get my name out."

"You'll get your name out soon enough," Ashleigh said. The phone rang, and she motioned for Mike to answer it. "You don't need to rush things."

"But I know I'm ready," Melanie protested. She tried to control her frustration. She certainly wouldn't convince her aunt and uncle of her maturity if she lost her temper. "This is what I've always wanted, and now I'm finally getting the chance to—"

Mike walked back into the dining room. The grim look on his face silenced Melanie. He handed the phone to his wife. "It's Christina. There's been an accident."

7

"HOW IS HE?" CHRISTINA DEMANDED AS SHE RAN INTO THE waiting room of the equine surgery clinic. "Have you heard anything?"

Patrick shook his head. "They're still in the early stages of what will be a long operation. Dr. John Reuter, one of the best equine surgeons in the country, is performing the surgery. I told him to do everything he could."

Christina stared at Patrick, barely able to understand what he was saying. Aaron led her to one of the plastic chairs, and she collapsed into it. "He has to be okay," she muttered. "He just has to." She looked at the clock on the wall of the waiting room. It had been over three hours since Callie had gone down. Aaron had forced her to get her wrist checked before taking her to the surgery clinic. The doctor had taken a couple of X rays before diagnosing it as a mild sprain and wrapping it in an Ace bandage. Strangely, it didn't hurt anymore.

The voices from the waiting room and the reception area faded in and out as Christina watched the clock. Nearly half an hour passed before she spoke again. "I—I should call home," Christina stammered. "My parents are hosting a dinner party, and I told them I would call after the race." Patrick handed her his cell phone. It took Christina three tries to dial the number correctly.

Her father answered the call. "Hi, Chris. How did you do today?"

Christina swallowed hard, trying to steady her voice. "Callie's hurt, Dad." She closed her eyes, remembering the moments after she and Callie had crossed the finish line. "The track vets said he shattered his sesamoids." Blood began roaring in her ears, making it hard for her to think. "I'm at the clinic now, waiting to hear about the operation."

For the next fifteen minutes Christina spoke with the other people who were at her house. Cindy talked the longest, telling Christina what she knew about Dr. Reuter. "He was a classmate of an old friend of mine, Max Smith," she said. "And a lot of the trainers I've worked for have used him before. He's done some amazing things, Christina."

Melanie got on the phone after Cindy. "I know

nothing will make you feel better until you know Callie will be all right, Chris, but you can't give up. You have to believe that Callie will make it, just like Raven and Image did."

Raven. The beautiful Whitebrook filly had also been injured because of Christina's negligence. "I have to go, Melanie," Christina said, feeling sick to her stomach. "Patrick needs his phone. I'll call back when I know more."

Christina handed the phone to Patrick and ran outside. She took deep, gasping breaths, trying to hold herself together.

This was all her fault. If she had pulled Callie up after that first stumble, then he wouldn't have put so much stress on the damaged ankle. Christina sank to the ground, putting her head in her hands. Why had she hesitated for so long?

The automatic doors opened. Aaron stepped outside. "Christina? Are you all right?"

"I'm fine," Christina managed to reply between gasps. She wiped her sweaty palms on her green-and-white silks.

"The doctor is coming out to talk to Patrick. I thought you might want to be there."

Christina clenched her left hand into a fist, feeling her fingernails dig into her palm. The physical pain did not lessen the emotional ache. "I'll be there in a minute," she said, still trying to slow her breathing. She heard the automatic doors close behind Aaron and felt relieved that he wasn't going to push her to talk.

"Pull yourself together, Chris," she mumbled to herself. "You can't do anything when you're like this." She crossed her fingers, hoping the vet would say that Callie's injury wasn't as bad as it had looked. But deep down Christina knew that vets didn't usually interrupt operations to give good news.

Aaron handed her a cup of water as she sat down. Christina shook her head. "I'm fine," she repeated, ignoring Aaron's concern.

A tall blond man walked through the double doors. His mint green scrubs were liberally splattered with blood. Callie's blood.

Christina fought the urge to be sick. She swallowed hard, studying the doctor's blue eyes as though they might tell her what he was going to say.

Dr. Reuter turned to Patrick. "Your colt sustained multiple injuries to his legs during the race," he began. His voice had a sympathetic, soothing quality. There was no inflection to indicate whether the news was good or bad. "It appears that he aggravated an old tendon injury in his left leg, making him put more weight on his right leg during the race. His right ankle buckled under this strain."

Patrick spoke up. "The X rays showed that he damaged his sesamoids and his ligaments," he said evenly. "Will you be able to repair the injuries?"

"In all my years as a surgeon, I've never seen an ankle shatter the way his did," Dr. Reuter replied.

"There were bone fragments everywhere, though I managed to get most of these out during the initial stages of surgery."

"So is he going to be all right?" Christina asked, unable to bear the slow, clinical tone of the discussion.

Dr. Reuter glanced toward her. "From what I've heard, the way you stopped Callie at the end of the race was the only thing that gave him a chance." Before Christina could repeat her question, the vet turned back to Patrick. "About an hour ago, your horse started to fight the sedation. When we increased his anesthesia, his heart stopped beating. We were able to revive him with electric shocks and epinephrine, but his rhythm is still unstable."

"Then you'll have to continue the operation with only low levels of sedation," Patrick concluded.

"We have yet to reconstruct the damaged bone and ligaments," Dr. Reuter said. His jaw was set now, making his expression grimmer. "It will take six to twelve hours for us to do this, and because we must be very careful about Callie's anesthesia levels, there is a large chance he will keep fighting the sedatives."

Image fought the sedatives after the Kentucky Derby, Christina thought furiously. *Image is still alive.*

"I think you have a difficult choice to make," Dr. Reuter continued softly. "I must be honest. Even if we work to the best of our capabilities, Callie will spend the rest of his life in terrible pain. I'm not sure he will ever be able to put weight on his leg again."

Patrick nodded slowly. "Are you suggesting that we stop the operation?"

"I'm suggesting that you think about how much suffering you want your horse to endure," Dr. Reuter answered.

"You can't give up on him!" Christina cried defiantly. Her heart pounded in her throat. "We can work him in a therapy pool. He won't have to put any weight on his ankle until it's recovered."

"I'm sorry, but there is no chance of a meaningful recovery," Dr. Reuter said gently.

"What do you mean?" Christina asked unsteadily.

"Callie would have to be confined in a stall. He would be unable to walk for more than a few minutes at a time."

Each of Dr. Reuter's words pressed against Christina's chest, releasing the sobs that she had held in check. Christina closed her eyes, feeling tears squeeze out from between her lashes. Racehorses couldn't live like that. No matter how much she wanted to keep Callie alive, she knew it would be wrong to sentence him to that fate.

Patrick picked up his cell phone. "I'm going to call the colt's owner."

Aaron put a hand on Christina's shoulder as Patrick talked with Marisa. Christina shook him off. She didn't deserve comfort.

She looked up at Dr. Reuter, glaring at him through the blur of tears in her eyes. He was supposed to be one of the best. How could he not find a way to save Callie?

Half listening to Patrick's conversation, Christina could tell that the trainer had gotten Marisa to agree to euthanasia. "Yes, of course, Marisa. He'll feel no pain," Patrick assured.

"Can we see him one last time?" Christina asked, her voice cracking.

There was a pause as Dr. Reuter considered her request. At last he said, "I don't think that's a good idea. He's in too much pain to recognize anyone."

Christina felt warm tears leaking out of the corners of her eyes. She did not bother to wipe them away. Instead she stood, walking over to the far window so that no one could see her face. "Good-bye, Callie," she whispered. "You were one of the fastest and bravest horses I've ever ridden." The tears came harder now, and choking sobs escaped past the lump in her throat. "I'm sorry, Callie. I'm sorry I failed you."

The red numbers glowed in the dark: 12:54.

Christina pulled the covers closer as she stared at the clock. Six hours had passed since Callie's death.

Aaron had taken her back to the motel. She had gone straight to her room, locking the door behind her. On autopilot she had called home, telling her parents Callie had died. They must have said something in reply, but Christina couldn't remember a word of the

81

conversation. Even now all she could hear was Dr. Reuter's grim prognosis.

I'm sorry, but there is no chance of a meaningful recovery.

Christina had started shaking uncontrollably after she got off the phone with her parents. She was still shaking now.

Even if we work to the best of our capabilities, Callie would spend the rest of his life in terrible pain.

Every time Christina closed her eyes she saw Callie lying on the track, suffering. Because she had not stopped him after his first stumble, Callie had suffered. Because she had been unable to hold him when the vets came, Callie had suffered more.

Christina threw back the covers, knowing she could not sleep. Shivering, she made her way unsteadily toward the bathroom sink and used her left hand to splash warm water on her face. Her right wrist had begun to throb dully. But that was nothing compared to the horrible, aching emptiness.

Christina turned away from the bathroom mirror and stared into the dark room. The only lights were the red numbers of the clock and the blinking message indicator on the phone.

The phone had rung several times. Christina had made no move to pick it up. Talking could provide a distraction. It might give her some sort of comfort. She was unworthy of comfort.

"I killed Callie," Christina whispered hoarsely. "I killed him."

Why hadn't she pulled Callie up when she had felt him bobble down the stretch? Why had she let her desire to win get in the way of her instincts?

The worst part was that no one blamed her. Dr. Reuter had even tried to praise her for her actions after the race. How could the doctor have given her any credit for helping Callie when she was the one who had made him run on his injured leg?

Christina gripped the porcelain tightly as white spots began blurring her vision. She forced herself to swallow, to breathe, but weakness and nausea washed over her anyway, leaving her cold and clammy.

Being a jockey was about putting the horse first. She had learned that long ago by riding claimers at Churchill Downs. Back then she had not hesitated when she thought a horse was injured. She had hesitated today. And now Callie was dead.

Christina went back into the other room and collapsed on her bed, curling up in a tight ball.

Callie would have to be confined in a stall. He would be unable to walk for more than a few minutes at a time.

Patrick and Marisa had found the compassion to save Callie from that life. She had not found the skill to save him from pain in the first place.

"I killed Callie," Christina whispered again. "How can I call myself a jockey when I killed him?"

8

"WELCOME TO NEW YORK. PLEASE WAIT UNTIL THE AIRCRAFT
has come to a complete stop at the gate and the seatbelt
sign has been turned off before moving about the
cabin."

Melanie ignored the flight attendant's instructions,
unbuckling her seatbelt and putting away the copy of
the *Daily Racing Form* she had been trying to read during the flight. She'd sat between Ashleigh and Cindy
on the airplane, but no one had said much.

Ashleigh had booked the first available flight after
hearing that Callie was dead. Melanie had insisted on
going with her aunt. She still didn't know what to say
to Christina. If Image had died after the Kentucky
Derby, there would have been no words to comfort her.

Ashleigh tried to make idle conversation as they

84

walked to the baggage claim area. She asked Cindy about Rush Street, who was scheduled to leave on a flight the next morning.

"I think he's ready for the Suburban," Cindy replied. "Ben decided to put Double Agent, a two-year-old by Champion, on the plane as well. There are some good maiden races in the upcoming weeks. I was thinking about—" Cindy stopped when she saw Ian standing by the baggage carousel. She hurried toward him, giving him a hug. "How's Christina doing?"

"She came down to the track this morning to tell me her wrist was too stiff for her to ride," Ian replied worriedly. "I asked her if she wanted to come to the airport, but she told me she wasn't feeling well and wanted to sleep."

Sleep? Melanie doubted her cousin was telling the truth. Most likely Christina was replaying the race in her head, wondering how she could have changed the outcome.

The drive to Belmont Park was subdued. Ian and Ashleigh kept up a superficial chatter about the Whitebrook horses. Charisma, a two-year-old filly, was the horse Ian was most excited about. A daughter of Star's half brother Wonder's Pride, Charisma had been training well at Belmont and had recently clocked two black-type works. She was entered in the Astoria Stakes, a small stakes race that would be run on Wednesday.

"Do you want to ride her, Melanie?" Ashleigh asked.

Melanie stopped staring out the window. "Christina usually rides Charisma," she replied. "You should probably ask her first."

Ashleigh nodded. "I just don't want to push Christina if she doesn't feel up to riding."

Would Christina feel like riding? Melanie couldn't imagine her cousin staying away from the track for too long. However, Melanie still had flashbacks to Image's accident every time she rode in a race. What would it be like for Christina?

Ashleigh's cell phone rang as Ian parked the car at the motel. She checked the number and handed it to Melanie. "It's Jazz."

Dr. Seymour had gone to Townsend Acres to check on Image that afternoon. Jazz had promised to call with the results. Melanie answered the phone anxiously as she got out of the car. "Hi, Jazz. What did the vet say?"

"Don't worry. It was mostly good news," Jazz replied. "How's your cousin?"

"I don't know. We're just outside her motel room now," Melanie said. She squinted through the darkness, watching Ashleigh, Ian, and Cindy knock on Christina's door.

"Why don't you go see Christina first?" Jazz suggested. "I'll call you back in an hour, and we can talk about Image then."

Christina had let the others in. Melanie was anxious to see her cousin, but she also wanted to know what Dr. Seymour had said. "Can you just tell me quickly?" she asked, walking toward the motel room.

"You know nothing with Image is ever quick," Jazz answered gently. "It will be easier if we talk later. Hang in there, Mel. And tell Christina that I'm thinking about her."

Jazz's sweet concern made Melanie smile. "I will, Jazz. Talk to you soon." Melanie hung up the phone and walked through the half-open door to Christina's room.

The motel room was dark except for a dim light on the nightstand. Christina was sitting on her bed. She looked terrible. Her face was a sickly shade of pale, making her red-rimmed hazel eyes seem startling in comparison. "Hi, Mel," she said softly. "How was your flight?"

"The usual," Melanie answered. Unable to stand the darkness, she flicked on the overhead light. Christina winced at the brightness. Judging from the dark, puffy circles under Christina's eyes, Melanie doubted that her cousin had slept at all. "It looks like we're going to be roommates at the track again," she said with false cheerfulness. "Dad and Susan are out of town, and I didn't want to stay at the house by myself."

"That's great," Christina said flatly.

"We're heading over to the track to check on the horses. Want to come?" Ashleigh asked.

Christina shook her head. "No, thanks. I'll just visit

them tomorrow." She turned back to Melanie. "How's Image? You never told me how she did when you walked her on soft ground."

"She did well," Melanie replied carefully. How could she talk about Image's improvement when Callie had died? "Dr. Seymour checked on her this afternoon." Melanie tried to make eye contact with Christina, but her cousin flinched away from her gaze.

"What did he have to say?"

"I wasn't there, but Jazz is going to call me later with an update." Melanie crossed her fingers, hoping for the best. "I'll let you know what he tells me."

Christina gave her a forced smile. "I'm sure it will be good news. Maybe you'll be able to bring her back to Whitebrook soon." Christina lay back down. "I don't want to be rude, but I should probably go to bed. Would you mind if we talked after the workouts tomorrow?"

"Of course not. But are you sure you should be riding with your wrist injury?" Ashleigh asked with motherly concern.

"It doesn't hurt," Christina replied sharply. "I'll be fine. I just need a good night's sleep." She pulled the covers over her head.

"I wish there was something we could do," Melanie said after Ashleigh had closed the door.

"It'll take some time before she's able to talk about it," Cindy replied. She had a faraway look in her blue eyes. "It's one thing to lose a horse, but to lose a horse the way she did . . . She's probably still in shock." Cindy blinked, and her eyes focused on Melanie again. "I'll talk to Dr. Reuter tomorrow and see if he can think of anything that might make Christina feel better. In the meantime I'll keep an eye on her."

"We all will," Ashleigh assured Melanie. "Now let's get to the track."

After greeting the Whitebrook horses and feeding them some carrots, Melanie went for a walk along the backside to wait for Jazz's call. When she reached barn four, she saw Amanda Johnston taking Blue Streak out of his stall. She hesitated, not sure whether the trainer wanted to talk just then.

Amanda waved, making Melanie's decision for her. Melanie walked over and petted Blue Streak, feeding him the last of her carrots. "How is he doing?" Melanie asked. The gray colt was prancing at the end of the lead line and spooking at the evening shadows.

"He's his usual energetic self," Amanda said. "I couldn't relax in our hotel room, so I decided to take some of our horses for a walk." The trainer looked down at Melanie. "I didn't know you were coming back so soon. Did you move up your flight because of Christina?"

Melanie nodded. "I thought she might want someone to talk to, and we've been through a lot together."

"Is she feeling better? Patrick said she looked ready to collapse when Aaron took her home last night."

"I'm not sure," Melanie replied, unable to lie.

89

"Has she talked to you about the race?"

"I don't think she's ready yet."

"Well, according to the surgeon, her actions at the finish line were what gave Callie a chance in the first place," Amanda said. The trainer shook her head. "It doesn't seem fair. Callie was such an amazing horse. When we bought him for Marisa at the Keeneland fall auction, I just knew he would be something special. He always tried his best. It didn't matter if he was running in a sprint or a distance race."

Melanie looked at the ground, not knowing what to say. She had never ridden Callie. She had only heard about him through Christina.

"Deborah, our assistant trainer, is flying out with our newest auction purchase tomorrow," Amanda continued after a pause.

"What's his name?" Melanie asked politely.

"Enigmatic. He's a two-year-old by Charismatic."

Now Melanie understood why Amanda was telling her about the new horse. The entire Thoroughbred world had watched Charismatic falter at the Belmont finish line. The great horse had hurt his ankle, just as Callie had. But Charismatic's injury had not been life-threatening.

"I saw what happened to your filly after the Kentucky Derby," Amanda said. "You must be thinking about that now."

"Image and Charismatic were lucky," Melanie replied, talking more to herself than to the trainer.

90

"Most accidents in horse racing don't have such happy endings." Once again Melanie replayed Image's accident in her head. What if she hadn't stopped Image from standing on her broken leg? What if the break hadn't been as clean? What if Image had fought the sedation even more? What if Brad hadn't offered to help? There were too many other possibilities.

"Patrick told me that even if Dr. Reuter had completed the operation, there still wouldn't have been a happy ending. Callie's injuries were too severe. He would have needed painkillers for the rest of his life, and even then he would have been unable to walk."

Melanie stifled a gasp at that revelation. The decision to put Callie down had been the only humane one. If Image had been faced with a life of pain and confinement after the Kentucky Derby, Melanie would have made the same choice.

"Anyway, I'm going to ask Christina if she wants to ride Enigmatic for us," Amanda continued. "If she decides she isn't ready for that, would you be willing to try him?"

"Sure," Melanie agreed. "But I can't imagine Christina turning down that—" The phone rang, interrupting Melanie and startling Blue Streak. "I'm sorry, but I should probably take this."

Amanda used a few quick tugs of the lead rope to stop Blue Streak from bucking. "No problem. Good night, Melanie. I'll see you at the track."

Melanie said a polite farewell and waited until

Amanda was out of earshot before she answered the call. "Hey, Jazz. Thanks for calling back."

"No problem. How's Christina?"

"She's pretty shaken up," Melanie replied. "I'm worried about her. She seems determined to avoid talking about the accident, and I'm not sure I want to be the one to bring it up."

"Don't force her to discuss the race. She needs time to come to terms with it on her own. Just be there for her when she finally decides she wants to talk about it."

"That's what everyone says, but I can't stand seeing her so upset." Melanie sighed. "I just wish I could make things better. Anyway, I could really use some good news. What did Dr. Seymour tell you?"

"He said that Image is healing far better than anyone could have predicted. He thinks that we'll be able to increase her daily walking time steadily over the next few months and that Image might even be trotting by the end of the summer."

Melanie let out a breath she hadn't realized she was holding. "That's wonderful."

"I also asked him when we could move Image back to Whitebrook," Jazz continued. "Dr. Seymour advised us to wait. He thinks Image could use more time in the therapy pool. He's also worried that a change of scenery would be too stressful for her right now. We all know how Image reacts around trailers."

Moving Image had always been a challenge. The filly hated trailers and tended to act up when she was within a hundred feet of one. "How much longer did Dr. Seymour recommend we keep her at Townsend Acres?"

"At least another month."

"Can you afford that?" Melanie was almost afraid to ask the question.

"I'll figure something out," Jazz said after a pause.

"Maybe you should talk to Brad again," Melanie suggested.

"We already know what his solution is going to be."

"I don't want to give up Image's first foal," Melanie replied. "But I don't want you to worry about how you're going to pay for the treatment she needs, either. There has to be another way." Moving Image back to Whitebrook earlier was out of the question. Melanie couldn't risk the filly's recovery. "Maybe I can offer him some more free jockeying or exercise riding."

"Do you have time for that?"

"It doesn't matter. Image is what matters." The words came out more sharply than Melanie had intended. She sighed. "I'm sorry, Jazz. I didn't mean to snap at you. I'm just not thinking straight anymore."

"Well, I don't think straight most days, so this makes us even."

Melanie laughed. "What did I ever do to deserve you?"

"I could ask the same question about you," Jazz replied. "Don't worry too much about Image while you're gone, Mel. I'll make sure they take good care of her."

"But aren't you busy with the band right now?" Jazz had at least four more stops on his East Coast tour.

"It's okay, Mel. Your job right now is to take care of Christina. Let me worry about Image."

Because Jazz was being so sympathetic, Melanie didn't force the issue. But her concerns about Image and Jazz lingered as she returned to her motel room. At some point soon they would be faced with a difficult choice. Image had to have the best treatment, even if it meant that Melanie wouldn't be able to train her beloved filly's first foal.

Although it was only nine-fifteen, the motel room was dark when Melanie returned. She unlocked the door quietly and clicked on one of the lamps. Christina had buried herself under the covers, and it was impossible to tell whether she was really sleeping.

Just in case she was, Melanie tried to make as little noise as possible as she prepared for bed. As she crawled under the covers Melanie's mind was racing too much for her to fall asleep. The day before, when Cindy had suggested that Melanie had a lot more to learn about the racing world, Melanie hadn't believed her. She had assumed that the grueling Triple Crown had taught her all that she needed to know.

But Callie's death had reminded Melanie of how differently Image's story could have ended. Image had been lucky. *Melanie* had been lucky. Did she have the experience to get her through difficult situations if her luck ran out?

9

"WE WANT HER TO LOOK SHARP TODAY," ASHLEIGH SAID AS
Christina tried to settle herself in Charisma's saddle.
The chestnut filly pranced in place, ready to start the
workout. "Jog her a couple of laps and then we'll do a
half-mile breeze."

Christina nodded tightly, trying not to betray how
daunting these simple instructions sounded. The track
seemed to stretch interminably before her. Looking
down at the dirt surface, Christina found it impossible
not to think about Callie lying there in pain.

As she eased Charisma onto the track Christina
tried to ignore her queasy stomach and pounding
head. She had gotten only a few hours of uneasy sleep
since Callie's death, and she felt awful.

Christina swallowed past the nervous tightness in

her throat. She reminded herself that, despite the mistakes she had made in the Riva Ridge Breeders' Cup, everyone at Whitebrook still expected her to behave like a jockey. In fact, Ashleigh had listed her as Charisma's jockey for that day's Astoria Stakes post position draw. But Wednesday seemed so far away. Christina didn't know if she could even make it through a workout.

Sensing her rider's uneasiness, Charisma danced sideways. Christina barely managed to correct the filly as they drifted to the inside, which was reserved for the breezing horses. "It's all right, girl," Christina said, her voice shaking.

Charisma jerked her head forward, pulling the reins through Christina's fingers. Small spasms of pain shot through Christina's right wrist as she tried to reposition her hands. Charisma took advantage of her rider's lack of control and broke into a canter.

Christina pulled back in small, sharp tugs. "Slow down, Charisma. Please slow down." But Charisma continued to push forward at a choppy canter, ignoring Christina's commands. Christina gritted her teeth. "You have to stop, girl," she muttered. "I can't let you get hurt, too."

The filly gave an energetic buck, nearly throwing Christina over her head. Christina tried to regain her balance as Charisma darted toward the inside again. As they rounded the clubhouse turn a horse breezed past them, nearly brushing Charisma's shoulder. The filly wheeled around before roaring into a flat-out gallop and chasing the other horse.

"No, Charisma!" Christina cried as she hauled desperately on the reins. Her hold was useless. Charisma was accelerating in huge bursts, determined to catch the other horse. Christina felt herself blacking out and had to grab hold of the filly's mane to stay in the saddle. Each time Charisma's front hooves hit the ground, Christina's stomach dropped. She could picture Charisma stumbling just as Callie had.

Charisma drew even with the other horse. As they flashed past the half-mile marker the other horse stopped. The exercise rider yelled at Christina, but she was too intent on stopping Charisma to hear what he said.

Now that she had beaten the other horse, Charisma slowed, dropping back to a ragged canter. "Good girl," Christina said shakily. Applying pressure with her inside leg, she forced Charisma back to the outer edge of the track. When they were out of the way of the breezing horses, she pulled back on the reins again, sighing with relief as the filly broke to a trot.

Both Christina and Charisma were breathing hard when they returned to Ashleigh. "I don't think I was ready to ride," Christina apologized, unable to look at her mother. "I probably ruined her chances for the Astoria."

"It wasn't your fault. The other horse should have

been watching where he was going," Ashleigh said, checking Charisma's legs. Now that the filly was standing, her breathing was slowing, but her coat was lathered with sweat.

"No, I let her drift to the inside," Christina protested. Under any other circumstances, she knew, her mother would have been scolding her for not paying attention. She didn't want special treatment because of Callie's death.

Ashleigh ran a hand down Charisma's back legs. "Well, there doesn't seem to be any harm done. Why don't you take her around again to cool her down?"

Christina could not bear the thought of circling the track again. "I—I can't," she stammered. "My—My wrist is still bothering me. You should have Mel work her. Actually, Mel should probably be her jockey on Wednesday, too."

"Charisma's your responsibility this morning. You should finish the workout," Ashleigh said firmly. "And I want you to be her jockey."

Christina shook her head. She held her wrist close to her side, pretending to be in more pain. "Please don't make me. It hurts too much to ride."

"Do you want me to take you to the doctor? We could—" Ashleigh stopped in midsentence as her cell phone began to vibrate. She answered it while taking hold of Charisma's head so that Christina could loosen her hold on the reins. "Hello? . . . Yes, she's right here."

Ashleigh motioned for Christina to dismount and then handed her the phone. "It's Monica Patankar from the Belmont stewards' office."

The stewards' office? Had the trainer of the horse that Charisma had chased lodged a complaint against her already? Christina put the phone to her ear, steeling herself for a reprimand.

"Good morning, Ms. Reese. I am calling on behalf of Pierre Hutchinson, Belmont's chief steward. He is in charge of the inquiry—"

"I'm sorry about what happened this morning," Christina interrupted. "I should have kept my horse under control."

"I'm not sure what you're referring to, Ms. Reese. The track officials would like to see you in their office at ten this morning to discuss Marisa Pavlik's inquiry into Calm Before the Storm's death."

Callie. Christina's breath caught in her throat. The stewards must have watched the race tapes and seen how she failed to pull Callie up after he bobbled down the stretch. "Yes, of course." Christina didn't realize she had spoken until she heard her voice echoing back over the cell phone. "I'll be there at ten."

"We're ready for you now, Ms. Reese."

The voice made Christina jump. Nervously she smoothed a fold in her skirt. She stood, following Mrs. Patankar into a conference room with a large rectangular table in the middle. Four people were seated on each side of this table, and Mrs. Patankar motioned for her to sit at the head. Christina tentatively slid into the large leather chair.

The committee members introduced themselves. The only name Christina remembered was Pierre Hutchinson's. The thin, twitchy chief steward sat on her right.

"Marisa Pavlik has asked us to investigate Calm Before the Storm's death after the Riva Ridge Breeders' Cup," Mrs. Patankar began briskly. "Ms. Pavlik believes that the trainers at Dreamflight Racing Farm may have rushed her horse back to the track after his earlier tendon injury."

Christina couldn't help gaping in disbelief. She had expected Marisa to blame her. Why would the owner accuse the Johnstons of wrongdoing?

"Ms. Reese, our records show that you exercised Calm Before the Storm two days prior to the race. Did you notice any signs of injury then?" Mr. Hutchinson asked.

Christina shook her head slowly. Her mother had encouraged her to take her time before each answer. "Callie was perfect in the workout." Christina stumbled slightly over the horse's name. "He clocked one of his better times."

"Did the trainers check his legs after the workout?" the man beside Mrs. Patankar asked.

"I think so," Christina replied. "The Johnstons

always check their horses after exercise. But I was getting on another horse at the time, so I can't say for sure."

Mrs. Patankar nodded, jotting something down on her notepad. "Tell us about the race."

Christina took a deep, shuddering breath. "The Johnstons wanted me to get Callie to the front right away," she began. She recited the memories as if they had happened to someone else. It was the only way she could talk without breaking down. "But we were boxed in at first, and Callie became frustrated."

"Did you notice any change in his gait?" Mrs. Patankar interrupted.

The words stuck in Christina's throat as she remembered how Callie had bobbled down the stretch. But even though she felt she needed to tell the stewards about this, she couldn't choke out any sort of reply.

"When we watched the tapes, we did not see any changes until the finish line," Mrs. Patankar said, growing impatient. "But as Callie's jockey, did you feel anything before then?"

Christina cleared her throat. "I think Callie's gallop became a little uneven down the stretch," she managed to say. "But he kept running strongly, so I didn't think anything was wrong." Christina looked down at the mahogany table. Her eyes traced the dark, swirling patterns in the wood as the stewards scribbled frantically. She waited for them to ask her why she hadn't suspected something was wrong.

Mr. Hutchinson was the first to finish writing. "Can you tell us what happened at the finish line?" he asked.

"When I felt Callie stumble, I knew I had to stop him," Christina replied. "He lurched across the finish line, obviously in pain, but he wouldn't slow down. I jumped off, trying to make him stop. He still refused. The other horses swerved past him, and I think that upset him even more. He wanted to chase them. I kept trying to calm him until the vets came."

"And that's when he went down, right?" Mrs. Patankar asked.

Christina nodded in confirmation. "I don't remember much after that," she mumbled. Of course, that was a lie, but Christina didn't think she could relive those details in front of the stewards.

"We've already spoken with Dr. Murphy and Dr. Stucker," Mr. Hutchinson said. He stood, extending his hand. "Thank you for coming in, Ms. Reese."

Christina looked at the head steward in surprise as she shook his hand. "Don't you have more questions?"

"Your account confirms what others have already told us," Mr. Hutchinson replied. "We'll be in touch if we need any more information. Before you go, however, I would like to tell you that I think what you did at the end of the race was very courageous. Few jockeys would have put themselves in such danger to save a horse."

Christina murmured what she hoped was an

appropriate response before leaving the room. Tears stung her eyes as she heard the door close behind her. After all the mistakes she had made in the race, she deserved punishment, not praise.

Numbly Christina walked down the hall, passing several rooms where apprentice jockeys were watching replays of races. She was glad the stewards hadn't forced her to sit through a replay of Callie's race.

What was she going to do for the rest of the day? She certainly couldn't go back to the track.

A door opened behind Christina, and she turned to see Amanda Johnston coming out of one of the offices. The trainer wore a navy blue business suit with a yellow blouse, and her hair was neatly brushed.

"Hello, Christina. I was hoping to catch you before you left," Amanda said, smiling tensely. "I met with the stewards earlier and told them that you did nothing wrong."

Christina stared at Amanda, momentarily frozen. Of course she had done something wrong. But maybe the Johnstons had as well. Perhaps they had rushed Callie back to the track after his tendon injury. After all, Dr. Reuter had said that Callie had reinjured a tendon in his left leg during the race, increasing the stress on his other leg and causing it to break.

"I've also talked with Marisa," Amanda continued. "She's mainly going through the inquiry for insurance purposes. She doesn't really blame any of us."

Christina looked away. Even if Marisa didn't

blame anyone, it didn't mean that no one was at fault. Had the Johnstons entered Callie in the race knowing that the colt was not sound? Had their negligence been responsible for Callie's bobble down the stretch? Suddenly Christina didn't want to be around Amanda anymore. "Um, excuse me, Amanda, but I should—I need to go to the track," she lied.

"Before you go, Christina, I wanted to tell you that Deborah flew in this morning with a colt that we bought at a California auction," Amanda said. "He's a two-year-old by Charismatic."

Christina flinched as she remembered her earlier conversation with Aaron. Charismatic's jockey had saved his mount. She hadn't saved hers. "I'm sure he's beautiful," she replied hollowly.

"His name is Enigmatic. He's still a little gangly, but we have high hopes for him. I was wondering if you wanted to be the first to ride him."

Christina's mind raced as she tried to come up with a polite answer. She wasn't ready to get on any horse just yet, especially not one the Johnstons were training. And if the stewards did find the trainers guilty, she didn't think she would ever be able to trust them again. "I'm not sure I have time for another horse," she mumbled.

"It shouldn't take too much time. We're going to take it easy at first," Amanda persisted. "We probably won't work him too hard until we get to Saratoga."

Christina shook her head. "I don't think I can right

now, but I'm sure Aaron or one of your other exercise riders would love the chance."

"Actually, your cousin agreed to ride him if you couldn't," Amanda told her. "But please let us know if you change your mind."

Christina barely heard Amanda's last words. How could Melanie have agreed to ride for Dreamflight without knowing the results of Marisa's inquiry? "I will," she managed to say, hoping her face did not betray her anger. "Thanks for the offer."

Christina waited until Amanda had started walking away before pushing through the glass doors. Although she did not want to see the track anymore, she stalked in that direction, searching for Melanie. She finally found her cousin outside Rush Street's stall with Cindy.

"Will you excuse us for a moment, Cindy?" Christina asked curtly.

Cindy looked surprised at Christina's tone. "Sure, but come find me later, Christina. I talked with Dr. Reuter this morning."

Christina winced at the mention of the surgeon. She nodded. "This shouldn't take long." She glared at her cousin, not caring what Cindy thought about her attitude.

"What's wrong, Chris?" Melanie asked once Cindy was a good distance away.

"How could you tell the Johnstons that you would ride for them?" Christina asked, venom dripping from her voice. "I had to go before the stewards today because they believe the Johnstons may have caused Callie's death."

Melanie took an involuntary step back. "I don't think that's true. Cindy told me what the vet said," she replied. "Dr. Reuter thinks that Callie's bones and ligaments in that ankle were naturally weak. What happened was a freak accident, Chris. No one could have prevented it."

"Callie was putting so much pressure on his right leg because he injured the tendon in his left leg again," Christina retorted. She closed her eyes, remembering how Callie had faltered down the stretch. "If Patrick and Amanda had given Callie more time after the first injury, then he might still be alive."

"Or maybe he would have broken his ankle in another race," Melanie pointed out. "The Johnstons waited over six weeks to race Callie after his injury. That's how long most trainers wait after a tendon strain. Callie's death was an accident, Chris. It wasn't anyone's fault. I'm sure that's what the stewards will decide."

"What if the stewards do decide that Callie's death was the Johnstons' fault?" Christina challenged. "Would you still ride for them then?"

"Probably not," Melanie replied. "But I really doubt the stewards will blame the Johnstons. It would be as ridiculous as blaming you for what happened."

Christina stared at her cousin, unable to believe

107

what Melanie had just said. "The stewards don't need to blame me," she choked out, blinking rapidly as she felt the familiar pressure of tears in her eyes. "I already know it's my fault." With that, she spun around and ran away.

Returning to her motel room, Christina made no effort to hold back her tears. She knew that she had been wrong to yell at Melanie. Since Christina wasn't sure yet whether she blamed the Johnstons for Callie's death, how could she expect her cousin to? But Melanie's final words had stung.

When Christina had crashed into another horse while riding Raven, one of Melanie's favorite White-brook horses, her cousin had been furious. Melanie had not spoken to Christina for days, blaming her for not paying enough attention. Christina had apologized, knowing Melanie was right. At the time she had been too focused on Star and the Triple Crown to think about much else.

The Triple Crown races were over now, yet Christina had made another horrible mistake. She had been too focused on winning to pull Callie up when she suspected an injury. What would Melanie think when Christina told her about this error? At least the vets had found a way to save Raven, putting her injured leg in a sling to let the tendons heal. Her mistake with Callie was irreparable.

Christina closed her eyes, seeing a nightmarish kaleidoscope of images behind her eyelids. Raven crashing in a race at Keeneland and going down . . . Image lying on the track after the Kentucky Derby . . . Callie stumbling before they crossed the finish line . . . over and over she saw the horses racing and getting hurt.

The phone rang. Christina picked it up to escape from the memories of track accidents.

"Hi, Chris. I've been trying to call since Saturday night." Parker's voice was soft with concern. "How are you?"

"I'm okay," Christina replied. She felt guilty about ignoring Parker's messages, but she wasn't sure she could handle another conversation about the accident. "Would you mind if I called you back, Parker? I've been up for almost two days straight, and I really need to sleep."

"Let's just talk for a few minutes first. I've missed you," Parker said. "Have you talked to anyone about what happened?"

"Well, I had to go before the stewards today," Christina answered flatly. "They think the Johnstons might have rushed Callie back from his injury."

"That's surprising. From what you've told me, they don't seem like the type of trainers who would do that."

"I don't know anymore," Christina said. Frustrated tears filled her eyes. She already knew the accident was her fault. But being able to blame the Johnstons eased a little of the guilt. So why was everyone insisting that the trainers had done nothing wrong? "All I know is that Callie's dead. Obviously all of us made mistakes."

"You can't think of accidents like that. You told me the same thing when Foxy nearly died of heat exhaustion after cross-country at the Rolex."

Christina remembered the incident from the previous spring. Parker had pushed his horse too hard despite warnings about the heat, and Foxy had nearly collapsed. "But Foxy's still alive. You didn't kill her like I killed Callie."

"You didn't *kill* Callie," Parker said. "Knowing you, you probably did everything you could to save him."

Christina's fragile temper snapped. "You don't know anything about what happened in that race! You have no idea what it's like to know that you could have saved a horse but didn't!"

"Listen, Chris, I didn't mean to—"

"I know," Christina interrupted. "I just wish everyone would stop talking to me about the race. I need some time to think about things alone."

"Do you want me to hang up for now?" Parker asked.

Christina knew that she would start reliving the race again once she put down the phone, but she couldn't think of anything else to say to Parker. "Yes, please. I'll talk to you later."

Parker sighed. "Good-bye, Chris. I love you."

"Good-bye, Parker." Christina heard a click as Parker hung up. She kept the phone against her ear until she heard the harsh beeping that indicated it was off the hook.

Setting the phone down on the cradle, Christina wondered what she was going to do now. A year ago she had fallen in love with the racing world because of the excitement that came with helping young Thoroughbreds achieve their potential. She wasn't sure that was what racing was about anymore. How could she believe that being a jockey was the best way to work with horses after what had happened to Callie?

And if she no longer believed in what she was doing on the track, then how could she choose jockeying as a career?

10

Enigmatic behaved like all two-year-olds did in the early stages of their training. The colt spooked at odd sounds, tried to run out at each of the sweeping turns, and jerked his head when she pulled on the reins.

"That's a good boy, Enigmatic," Melanie praised after they had circled the track two times at a jog. Amanda had asked her to take it slowly, wanting to give the colt time to adjust to his new environment. A rueful smile crossed Melanie's face as she tried to figure out what this horse's nickname would be. *Enigmatic* was a mouthful, but how could it be shortened? Iggy? No, that was too silly. Matt? Dreamflight already had a Matt. Enigma? Maybe.

It was good to have something to smile about. Since Christina had confronted her the day before,

Melanie had been trying to come up with a suitable reply. Melanie could understand why Christina thought the accident had been her fault. After all, Melanie still thought she was responsible for Image's injury. But she knew that Christina needed to get past blaming herself in order to heal.

That morning the stewards had told the Johnstons that they were dropping the investigation of Callie's death. Christina hadn't been on the track to hear that. She had stayed in the motel room, claiming that her wrist was still bothering her. Melanie knew Ashleigh had been in to talk with Christina, but judging from the worried expression on her aunt's face during the workouts, she guessed it hadn't done much good.

As Melanie guided Enigmatic back to the Johnstons, she felt guilty about riding for the trainers. It wasn't because she believed they were responsible for Callie's death. It was because riding for the Johnstons had originally been Christina's opportunity. Her cousin should have been the one taking Enigmatic around the track this morning.

"How was he?" Patrick asked, taking Enigmatic's reins.

"His gaits were smooth, and he has a sweet personality," Melanie replied. She thought back to Image's two-year-old training. The filly's personality had been described in many ways. *Sweet* hadn't been one of them.

Would Image pass her personality on to her foals?

Had Charismatic passed his on to Enigmatic?

Melanie considered Brad's idea of breeding Image to Celtic Mist. The foal would have Alydar, Seattle Slew, and Affirmed in its pedigree. Although blood-lines alone didn't make a great racehorse, it would be exciting to know that so much potential was there. But if she let Brad have this foal, then she would never get the chance to know and to train it.

"Why don't you ride Matt next?" Patrick said as Melanie dismounted. "I was hoping Christina would be feeling well enough to breeze him today. He needs a good work to stay in shape for the Suburban."

"Christina's just playing it safe so that she can ride in the weekend races," Melanie lied. "I'm sure she'll be back tomorrow or the day after that." Melanie crossed her fingers, hoping this was true.

"If she isn't ready, do you have a mount for the Suburban?"

Melanie nodded. "I'm riding Rush Street for Tall Oaks," she replied. "But don't worry, Christina will be able to ride." It would be her job to make sure of it.

Melanie guided Matt around the track several times before breezing the horse for five furlongs. Matt's personality reminded her of Image's. He was constantly testing his rider and fighting restraint. When Melanie finally gave the horse his head, though, he ran eagerly, his long legs eating up the track.

Aaron was standing with Patrick on the rail when Melanie finished this breeze. He waited until Patrick had finished talking to Melanie and a groom had led Matt away before approaching her.

"How's Christina?" Aaron asked. "I've been calling her room, but she won't answer."

"She's not doing very well," Melanie admitted. "The meeting with the stewards shook her up even more."

"But the stewards said that the accident wasn't anyone's fault."

Melanie shook her head. "Christina doesn't believe that."

"It's the truth." Aaron slammed his hand against the rail for emphasis. "I've watched the race tape a thousand times. There wasn't anything Christina could have done to change what happened."

"Do you still have the tape?" Melanie asked, an idea forming in her mind.

"Yeah. Do you want to see it?"

Melanie nodded. "But I want Christina to be there, too."

An hour later Melanie unlocked the door to the motel room. Christina was awake, flipping through a college catalogue, but she turned away when the door opened.

"Hey, Chris, look who followed me home," Melanie said cheerily.

Aaron stepped into the room. "Hi, Christina."

Christina slowly looked toward them. The circles

under her eyes were darker and more swollen now. Her wrist was still wrapped in a bandage, but she had been using that hand to turn pages in the catalogue. "How are you, Aaron?" she asked softly.

"I'm all right," Aaron replied. He held the tape out to her. "I have something I want you to see."

Christina closed her eyes, pushing the tape away. "I can't watch the race," she said, her voice trembling. "Not if it means seeing Callie . . ."

Ignoring Christina's protests, Melanie began connecting the VCR she had borrowed to the motel television. After the Kentucky Derby she had watched the race tape obsessively, wanting to know if Image had shown any signs of injury before going down. But would she have felt the same way if Image had not survived? "I'll make you a deal, Chris," Melanie said. "Let's watch this once. If you can show me why you think the accident was your fault, then I'll give Aaron back the tape and leave you alone."

There was no reply. Melanie took the tape from Aaron and hit the play button.

As the horses appeared on the screen Melanie watched her cousin carefully. Christina remained motionless. Only her hazel eyes flickered as they caught on Callie's image.

Melanie tried to watch the race through a jockey's eyes. At the beginning Christina and Callie had been boxed in. Melanie could tell Callie had given Christina a hard time as her cousin tried to find running room.

Christina had finally taken him through a narrow gap along the rail.

After that, Callie took off as though he had been shot from a cannon. He passed horse after horse almost effortlessly. It looked as though Callie was going to catch the first-place horse, Congress of Vienna, until the colt stumbled a few yards from the finish line. Christina stood in the stirrups, but Callie did not slow until he passed the finish line.

Melanie turned back to Christina, seeing tears in her cousin's hazel eyes. "Callie was bred to win. Of course you couldn't stop him so close to the finish line."

Christina shook her head, wiping her eyes with the back of her hand. "That wasn't the first time he stumbled," she whispered. Her eyes were fixed on the stilled image of Callie hobbling across the finish line.

"What do you mean?" Melanie wondered whether this was what Christina had been obsessing over for the past few days. "Callie's strides were even until just before the finish." Melanie replayed the final seconds of the race in her head, unable to remember anything unusual except Callie shaking his head several times in the final furlong. Had Christina been trying to stop him then?

Christina's shoulders began to shake. "He bobbled down the stretch," she choked out. "I tried to pull him up, but he wouldn't stop." Christina closed her eyes and pressed her palms against them. "And then I

117

began to think that the Johnstons and Callie's owner would be angry with me if I cost Callie the race for no reason, so I let him keep running." She buried her face in her hands. "Callie's dead because I didn't want him to lose."

Melanie put a hand on her cousin's back. "I would have made the same decision."

Christina moved away angrily. "But you didn't!" Her voice had a hysterical edge to it. "You don't have to live with the knowledge that you killed a horse."

Melanie started to speak again, but Aaron interrupted her. "Let's see the end of the race again, Christina. I want you to show me where you felt that bobble." He rewound the tape back to the point where Callie shot through the gap on the rail.

Melanie focused on Callie's front legs during this replay, watching his galloping strides for signs of lameness. She couldn't find any.

Aaron paused the tape just before Callie crossed the finish line. "I didn't see anything. Did you, Melanie?"

Melanie shook her head.

"He stumbled," Christina murmured. "I was there. I felt it." She stood abruptly, walking over to the window and sliding into the corner. Drawing her knees up to her chest, she began to cry.

Forgetting about the tape, both Melanie and Aaron moved toward Christina. They sat down on either side of her.

"Even if I can't pick out the exact moment, it doesn't mean that nothing happened," Christina said. She pressed her hands to her mouth to muffle her sobs. "The vet said that Callie hurt his tendon again. What if the bobble I felt was that injury? Callie could have kept running through it, but the stress he put on his other leg got to be too much."

"Maybe that's what happened," Melanie replied, feeling helpless in the face of Christina's grief. "But the stewards and vets have studied the race and Callie's injuries. None of them have a definite conclusion about what caused the injury."

"I don't care what any of them say. They weren't riding Callie in the race. They didn't feel that bobble. They weren't there when I lost my hold on Callie's reins. They didn't have to watch Callie go down on the track in pain. I keep wondering . . ." Christina's sobs drowned out the rest of her words.

"You keep wondering if you could have done something to prevent what happened," Melanie guessed. That was the question that had compelled her to watch the tape of the Kentucky Derby so many times.

Christina nodded. "If I could just understand why all this happened, then maybe I could move on," she said desperately. "Maybe I could ride again. Or maybe I could believe what everyone is telling me."

"What if the only explanation is that Callie died because of a horrible combination of circumstances?" Aaron asked.

"If that's the case, then I contributed to the circumstances," Christina replied dully.

"And so did I," Aaron pointed out. "I was the first person to ride Callie after his injury. Maybe something happened then that contributed to his breakdown during the race."

"You never noticed anything that suggested he was still injured," Christina protested. "If you had, then you wouldn't have let him keep running."

"But you tried to stop him when you thought something was wrong," Aaron said. He put a hand on Christina's shoulder, making her look at him. "We both know what it was like to ride Callie. When he decided to run, it was almost impossible to hold him back. Nothing you did or didn't do would have made him stop before crossing the finish line."

Christina stared at Aaron with bloodshot, tear-filled eyes for several long moments before she spoke again. "Can I have some time to myself?"

Melanie exchanged glances with Aaron. She didn't want to leave her cousin alone, but what more was there to say?

"I know what you two wanted to show me, and I'm glad you came," Christina continued hoarsely. "And I will talk to you later. I won't keep hiding. Really. I just need some time to think."

Aaron stood, briefly touching Christina's shoulder again. He walked past the television, taking the tape out of the VCR.

"I'll be back in a few hours. Call if you need anything," Melanie said before she followed Aaron outside.

"Do you think we got through to her?" Aaron asked once the door was closed.

"I hope so," Melanie replied. She watched as Aaron fidgeted with the tape, turning it over in his hands. "I think it was good for her to see the race. Nothing we showed her could have been worse than the replays in her head." Melanie shuddered involuntarily as she remembered the flashbacks she'd had after Image's accident. "What you said at the end probably made the biggest difference."

"That's because I used those arguments to convince myself first." Aaron looked down at the ground. "I had to think about what happened to Callie as an awful, random accident—a product of too many factors to count. Otherwise I wouldn't have been able to set foot on the track again." Aaron cleared his throat before giving Melanie a small smile. "Christina will come around," he said with forced conviction. "She's too good a jockey to stop racing because of this."

Even with all that was going on, Melanie somehow managed to ride a Whitebrook horse, Finding Faith, to victory that afternoon. After that win she joined her aunt and Cindy in the grandstand. But her mind wasn't on the races, and she went back to her motel room much earlier than usual.

Christina was sitting on her bed, still reading the college catalogue. The television was on, but she was paying more attention to her book than the program. "Feel free to turn that off," Christina said as Melanie tossed her bag onto the floor. "It was just too quiet in here."

Melanie studied Christina's face as she switched off the television. Her cousin's skin was still pale and her lips were pressed tightly together, but her eyes seemed a little less red and dull. "I'm sorry if Aaron and I pushed you this morning," Melanie began. "We shouldn't have made you watch that tape until you were ready to see it." She sighed. "I mean, I've been thinking about Callie's race since I saw that tape, so I can imagine what it's like for you."

"It's okay, Mel," Christina replied. "It felt good to talk to you and Aaron about the race. But even if no one else saw Callie bobble, I'm still convinced that it happened. And I just wish everyone would stop telling me how I'm supposed to feel about that. I can't go back to the track and pretend the accident didn't happen."

"But you also can't stop jockeying because of a mistake you think you made in one race. You're too good at it," Melanie said, echoing Aaron's earlier words. "I know you've been thinking about other careers lately and looking into college classes, but you can't let this accident make the decision for you."

Christina closed the catalogue. "I won't stop racing

just because of Callie. There are other reasons for me to be a vet. Look at what happened to Raven and Image, or think about Star's illness."

Star had been very sick the previous fall. He probably would have died had it not been for Christina's determined care. "What you've done with the horses proves you would be a great vet, Chris," Melanie said. "I just know you could be a great jockey, too. And I can't imagine trying to qualify for my professional license without you competing with me," she added teasingly.

"But I thought you wanted to leave Whitebrook and try to make it on your own."

"I'm not so sure about that anymore," Melanie admitted. She sat down at the edge of Christina's bed. "When I saw the tape of Callie's race, I realized once again how lucky Image was. And that made me think of how many lucky breaks I've gotten in my jockeying career. If your mom and dad hadn't been so supportive and given me rides at the beginning, or if Jazz hadn't bought Image, then I wouldn't be where I am today."

"You earned all of that," Christina said. "You made Image a champion."

Melanie shrugged. "I did the work, but there was still luck involved. I know you always need luck in horse racing, but maybe I'll need a little less if I learn more about how the racing world works. And I can't think of better people to learn from than your parents and Cindy." Melanie picked up the catalogue Christina had been looking at and opened to a random page. It was a listing of chemistry courses. She made a face. "Are you sure chemistry would be more interesting than jockeying?"

"I'll need chemistry classes for vet school," Christina said. "I'm not ready to register for any until I learn more about being a vet, though."

Melanie read through the class titles, unable to find one that looked remotely interesting. This was where she and Christina differed. She couldn't understand how her cousin could want to go back to class when she was finally free to ride all the time.

"I've been talking to Cindy about my decision," Christina continued. "She arranged for me to spend tomorrow afternoon at the equine surgery clinic where they worked on Callie."

Melanie looked up in surprise. "Are you sure you're ready to go back there?"

Christina nodded slowly. "I can't hide forever from what happened." She sighed. "Remember how crazy things were back in March and April?"

Melanie nodded. She had been in Florida, preparing Image for the Florida Derby at Gulfstream Park. Back then she hadn't known whether Image would be competitive against colts, and the filly's temperamental disposition had caused so many problems on the track. "It seemed like the only things anyone could talk about at Whitebrook were Image, Star, and the Triple Crown."

"When I took Star to California, I thought that if I could just get past the Triple Crown, everything would work itself out," Christina said. "Now I see how wrong I was."

"Everything did work out for you and Star," Melanie pointed out. "You two got better with every race."

Christina lay back in her bed. She tucked her hands under her head and stared at the ceiling. "I love Star," she said. "But I'm starting to think that loving one horse might not be a good enough reason to stick with racing."

11

"THIS IS OUR ULTRASOUND MACHINE." DR. REUTER GESTURED through the observation window of the large corner room. A flat-screen monitor was connected to a complex series of machines. "Have you ever observed an ultrasound?"

Christina stood on her tiptoes for a clearer view. A technician was holding a nervous young Thoroughbred while the veterinarian ran a probe over its stomach. The monitor showed contrasting white, gray, and black shapes. "A few times," she replied. "The vets did one on my pony, Trib, when I was young." Christina tried to smile. Dr. Reuter had spent the past half hour showing her the facilities. At first she had been unable to listen because the sound of his voice reminded her of what he had said the day Callie died. She was still trying to get past that association.

"What was wrong with him?"

"The vet thought he heard a heart murmur, but it turned out to be nothing," Christina said. "I've also seen a few leg ultrasounds at the clinic in Lexington."

Dr. Reuter nodded. "We get a lot of these here. Trainers want to look at the tendons and tendon sheaths of their young racehorses."

Christina wondered whether an ultrasound of Callie's tendons had ever been done. Would that have made a difference?

Dr. Reuter continued down the hall. "Our X-ray rooms are on the left." He handed her a heavy beige apron. "I can't let you watch X rays being done if you don't wear one of these. The lead protects you from the radiation." He gestured to a small black badge that was clipped to the collar of his apron. "The vets and the staff also have to wear these. They measure the amount of radiation that we've been exposed to."

Christina draped the heavy apron around her, clumsily tying the strings at the back. When a horse needed X rays at Whitebrook, the vet usually brought a portable machine and shot the films at the barn. But those smaller machines didn't give the vets enough information for certain diagnoses. Most of the X rays being taken that day were leg films. But Christina also watched the vets take a series of spinal shots for one horse.

"Small-animal vets have it a lot easier when it comes to X rays," Dr. Reuter said after those films had been taken. "They can move their patients from the X-ray rooms even when they're still recovering from the anesthesia, but we can't exactly carry these horses around."

Christina laughed. "Did you ever think about small-animal medicine?"

"You study both in vet school," Dr. Reuter replied. He took off his lead apron and hung it on a hook in the wall. "I didn't make my decision until my third year, when I helped treat two horses that broke down in the same race. Seeing those horses in pain made me go into equine surgery. I wanted to be the one who could keep them from suffering." Dr. Reuter led Christina down another hall. "Do you want to see our main operating room? It's where we worked on your horse."

Christina took a deep breath. Dr. Reuter had not wanted her to go into that room the Saturday before because Callie had been in too much pain to recognize her. "Yes, I do," she answered at last.

The operating room was the largest room in the clinic. Christina stared at the sterile green floor tiles. She could almost picture Callie lying dead on this floor.

Dr. Reuter rolled a green gas cylinder toward her, fiddling with the black knobs. "This tank enables us to regulate the level of oxygen that a horse gets during surgery. Before an operation, we put a tube down the horse's throat and connect the tube to this machine. . . ."

Dr. Reuter's voice started to fade in and out as Christina imagined Callie with a tube down his throat. She bit her lip, forcing herself to focus as Dr. Reuter showed her another machine.

"We attach these electrical leads to the horses to monitor their heart rates." Dr. Reuter was holding some black wires that were attached to silver clips. "It's important to be aware of heart and respiratory rates during an operation. We have to be ready to adjust anesthesia and oxygen levels, to administer drugs, or even to shock the heart into beating again if something goes wrong."

Something had gone wrong during Callie's surgery. Dr. Reuter had probably used those electrical paddles to shock Callie's heart. Christina's chest tightened, and a darkening blur crept into the edges of her vision. It was getting harder and harder to breathe.

Dr. Reuter flipped a couple of switches, and the bright lights that were attached to swivels from the ceiling turned on. "You'll notice that everything in here can be moved quickly," he said. "That's important for an emergency. But even during routine operations, I'll change the angle of those lights so I can see the field better."

As Dr. Reuter moved one of the lights Christina's eyes caught its blinding flash. She closed her eyes, trying to clear her vision, but when she opened them again, the grayness was still there. Superimposed over this grayness was an image of Callie lying on the operating table as Dr. Reuter stood over him with blood-covered scrubs.

Suddenly it was as though all the air had been sucked from the room. Christina backed toward the door, trying not to panic. Her fingers clutched at the door frame, and she struggled to keep herself upright.

Dr. Reuter put an arm around Christina's shoulders, helping her into the hall. He waited patiently as she gasped for breath, her vision finally clearing. "I'm sorry," Christina managed to choke out as her composure returned. She felt her cheeks reddening with embarrassment.

"Don't be," Dr. Reuter replied simply. "Let's go to my office. I have some extra course catalogues from my vet school, and I want to give you one."

Christina was relieved that Dr. Reuter was not going to ask about her breakdown. As she walked down the hall she took some deep, calming breaths. Now that she was out of the operating room, the air no longer seemed so oppressive.

Dr. Reuter handed Christina a course catalogue as she sat down in one of the plush chairs facing his desk. Christina flipped through it for a few moments before closing it and putting it in her lap. "Did you always know you wanted to be a vet?" she asked at last.

Dr. Reuter shook his head, chuckling. "It took me forever to figure out what I wanted to be when I grew up," he joked. "Even after college I still wasn't sure. I actually spent a couple of years in the Peace Corps before applying to vet school."

"What else did you consider?"

"Teaching, research, human medicine—pretty much anything that involved science," Dr. Reuter replied. "Cindy tells me that you're debating between jockeying and being a vet."

Christina nodded. "I became a jockey so that I could work with Wonder's Star," she said. "During Star's two-year-old season, nothing mattered more than being his jockey. I didn't think I would ever want to do anything else. But then Star got sick last winter, and I started seeing all these horses break down on the track. Now I don't know if jockeying is what I want to do anymore."

Dr. Reuter poured himself a mug of coffee. "Would you like some?" When Christina shook her head, he added, "You'll learn to like coffee if you go to vet school. Luckily, you still have lots of time to figure out if that's what you really want."

Lots of time? At her graduation, Christina had felt as though everyone was pressuring her to pick her next path. "I thought I already knew what I wanted," Christina said. "It makes me nervous to think that I don't."

"You don't have to limit yourself yet. Explore all your options while you can," Dr. Reuter advised. "And until you're sure you don't want to be a jockey, you should keep riding on the track."

Christina looked down at the catalogue Dr. Reuter

had given her. She had avoided the track again that morning, still unable to face what had happened. "Can I ask you one more question, Dr. Reuter?"

"Let me guess. You want to know my opinion about what happened to Callie."

"You told us that you had never seen an ankle shatter like that," Christina said, remembering the vet's grim diagnosis. "What do you think caused it?"

"Callie probably put some additional stress on his right leg when he aggravated the old tendon injury in his left," Dr. Reuter replied. "However, that alone would not have caused such a break. He probably also had some congenital or genetic condition that weakened those bones."

"Does that mean he shouldn't have been racing?"

"Not necessarily," Dr. Reuter said. "The trainers had no way of knowing this, and I've seen many racehorses have successful careers even with weaker bones and tendons." Dr. Reuter pointed to the bookshelves against his wall. They were filled with thick reference books. "I told you earlier that I always wanted a career in science. All these books have to do with the science of veterinary medicine. But the more surgeries I do, the more I'm convinced that sometimes luck has more to do with the outcome than science."

"Why?" Like Melanie, Christina assumed that getting more practice at something would mean she'd rely less on luck rather than more.

"Several times in my career I've had cases where there's no logical explanation for the outcome. Sometimes I make saves that are medically impossible. Other times horses die inexplicably in the operating room," Dr. Reuter answered. "I also think about luck when I see an injury like Callie's. No one thing caused it, Christina. If the footing on the track hadn't been so hard or if he had aggravated his tendon injury a few seconds later or if he had switched leads at a different moment down the stretch, then maybe he wouldn't have broken his ankle or maybe the break would have been operable."

Christina took in a deep breath. A horrible combination of circumstances. Just as Aaron had said.

"You've probably had some races where either everything has gone your way or you've managed to win in spite of all that has gone wrong, haven't you?" Dr. Reuter asked.

Christina nodded. Star's Belmont win had definitely been a case of the latter. Star had been unable to break clear of the pack of horses until the very end.

"And you've probably had races where you could have won if just one thing had gone your way," Dr. Reuter continued.

Again Christina thought back to the Triple Crown, remembering how Star had come in last during the Kentucky Derby because she hadn't found room for him to run. "Yes, I have."

"I think luck plays into any job," Dr. Reuter said.

"But someday when I look back on what I've done here, it's going to be the sum total of all the cases I've worked on that matters, not any one good or bad day. I'm willing to bet that you will feel the same way about racing."

Christina was still thinking about Dr. Reuter's advice later that afternoon. She finally ventured onto the track, watching Melanie and Charisma win the Astoria Stakes.

"Didn't I tell you she ran like a colt?" Christina asked Melanie when they posed for the photo in the winner's circle.

"You were right," Melanie replied. "She runs a lot like Image did."

"We'll be happy if she does half as well," Ashleigh said, running a hand down the filly's sweaty red-gold coat. Charisma craned her neck around, lipping Christina's hair. "I think she's missed you, Chris."

Christina forced herself to smile. "I've missed her, too." Even though she had been away from the track for only four days, Christina did miss the morning workouts. She was still afraid she would panic and let a horse run away with her again if she tried to ride.

Fortunately, her mother did not press the issue further. Christina stayed at the racetrack for another three races. The second of these was Double Agent's maiden race. Melanie rode Double Agent to a third-place finish even though the colt slipped at the start. Excited about the placing, Cindy was already planning other races for her horse.

There was a message waiting for Christina when she got back to the motel room. "Hello, Christina. This is Deborah Easton from Dreamflight. Patrick and Amanda asked me to call you. They want to know whether you will still be available to ride Matt for the Suburban Handicap. Please let us know as soon as possible."

Christina listened to this message twice. She had lashed out at the Johnstons when she needed an outlet for her anger at Callie's death. Part of her had even wanted the stewards to conclude that the accident had been the trainers' fault. That way she would not have needed to blame herself for being unable to pull Callie up when he had bobbled.

But maybe the problem had been her need to assign blame. Other people had looked into the accident. None of them had found fault. Perhaps there really was no single explanation for Callie's death.

Christina had seen her share of crooked trainers over the past few years. Alexis Huffman, for example. Even before she had faked Speed.com's disappearance to conceal a potentially serious injury, Alexis had done her share of morally questionable things. She had repeatedly tried to sabotage Image's career and had given one of her employers bad business advice. Ralph Dunkirk, the head trainer at Townsend Acres, was another person Christina could never work for.

His harsh training tactics had nearly ruined Star as a yearling.

But most trainers Christina had ridden with had taught her so much. Vince Jones, one of the most prominent trainers in Kentucky, had given her mounts when she was just starting out, and he had recently worked with her at Celtic Meadows. There was also Cindy, who had been a mentor and had offered her many rides with Tall Oaks.

Finally Christina had to admit that the Johnstons had always been more than fair to her. Despite her limited jockeying experience, they had been willing to take a chance on her. They had even offered her a job at Saratoga.

Christina knew what she had to do. She picked up the phone.

The insistent ringing of the telephone woke Christina from a deep sleep. After she had called the Johnstons to let them know that she would ride Matt for them in the Suburban, she had sprawled out on her bed, falling asleep instantly.

"Hello?" Christina mumbled groggily. She sat up, relieved that sleep had finally eased the dull pounding in her head. She couldn't remember the last time she hadn't had a headache.

"Hey, remember me?" Parker's teasing voice made Christina smile.

"Of course I do," Christina said. She turned on the bedside lamp, wincing as her eyes adjusted to the light.

"How are you feeling?"

"A little better," Christina replied. "Sorry about Monday." Parker had not called since then. Christina hoped he wasn't angry.

"Well, I shouldn't have pushed you so hard. You were right when you said that I didn't know what you were going through," Parker said. "Anyway, what's been happening at the track?"

"Let's talk about you first. Have you heard about Foxy and Ozzie?"

"They're doing great," Parker answered. "One of the grooms calls almost every day with an update. I can't wait to see them again."

"When are you leaving?"

"Soon, I hope," Parker said. "But Dad's giving me some trouble. He's been in a foul mood since Celtic Mist lost the Belmont."

Parker had been fighting with his parents about eventing for as long as Christina could remember. "Can your grandfather help?" Clay Townsend was one of Parker's biggest supporters. He had bought Foxy for Parker at an auction and had paid for his recent trip back to the United States.

"I'm trying to avoid dragging him into another family argument. It would be nice to stand up to my father on my own." Parker sighed. "I don't want to talk about this right now, Christina. I'm more worried about you."

"You don't need to worry anymore," Christina said. She told Parker about her conversation with Dr. Reuter and her decision to ride Matt in the Suburban. "I just hope I don't freeze when I'm on the track tomorrow."

"I wish I could make it better." Parker made a kissing noise over the phone.

Christina air-kissed him back. "Thanks for wanting to try. If you really wanted to help me out, you could decide what I should do for the rest of my life."

"Do you think you could work at a veterinary hospital?"

"Probably. Dr. Reuter and the other vets really believe in helping the horses. And I'd like to learn how to repair injuries like Image's or how to cure diseases like the one that almost killed Star. But if I want to go to vet school, then I would ultimately have to give up jockeying. I'm not sure I'm ready to do that yet." Christina twisted the phone cord in frustration. "I just wish I knew what I wanted."

"You don't have to figure it all out today," Parker said. "Can't you look into both careers for a while longer?"

"I plan to," Christina replied. "I want to go to college so that vet school is a possibility, but I think I'll stick with my original plan of starting classes next year. I've failed to follow through with so many things over the last few years." Christina had sold her first race-horse, Wonder's Legacy, to buy Sterling Dream, whom she had trained as an event horse. Then she had sold Sterling after she had gotten her jockey's license and started spending all her time with Star. "I can't add Star to the list, not after all we've been through together."

"That sounds like a good plan," Parker said. "Maybe I'll stop by Whitebrook and tell Star about it tomorrow."

Christina laughed. "Give him a carrot for me if you do." She missed the beautiful chestnut colt and couldn't wait until he was shipped to Saratoga. "In the meantime, I'll try to take a couple of classes at a community college. It wouldn't hurt to get a head start on all that science and math."

"You've never had any trouble before. I'm sure you'll be fine. Hold on a sec, Christina." Parker covered the receiver with his hand, and Christina heard the muffled sounds of his conversation. "I'm sorry, but I need to go. I promised Samantha I'd take care of the evening feedings tonight."

"Say hi to Sterling for me, then," Christina said. "Thanks for listening, even though I haven't been the best girlfriend lately."

"You're always the best girlfriend," Parker replied. "I love you."

Christina smiled. "I love you, too. Bye, Parker."

12

"READY TO GO?" MELANIE ASKED, LOOKING BACK AT Christina. She slowed Ending Shadows, a two-year-old colt, and waited for her cousin to catch up.

"Yes, let's warm them up," Christina replied, a nervous catch in her voice. She struggled to keep March to Honor, another two-year-old, from prancing sideways as she readjusted her gloves.

Ashleigh wanted Melanie and Christina to breeze the two-year-olds together in preparation for their maiden races. The farm had especially high hopes for March to Honor, a son of March to Glory and Honor Bright. Because of her connections with the colt's dam and sire as well as his sister, Honor and Glory, Cindy was also watching March to Honor closely.

Melanie kept glancing back at Christina while they cantered through the warm-up. Christina's announcement that she was going to ride Matter of Time in the Suburban Handicap had been a pleasant surprise. Not wanting to shatter Christina's fragile confidence, Melanie had refrained from asking whether she was sure about that decision.

Christina certainly looked more at ease than she had when exercising Charisma on Monday. But she was chewing at her lower lip and holding the reins more tightly than she needed to.

Both colts made it through the warm-up without incident. They tried to run out during the wide, sweeping Belmont turns, but both responded to their riders' corrections. Christina was the first to ask for a gallop, leaving Melanie to follow. The plan was for them to gallop their horses slowly to the far turn and then breeze them down the long homestretch.

Melanie's throat felt dry as they started galloping. For Christina's sake, this breeze had to go well.

The two colts approached the far turn, gaining speed. Melanie crouched forward over her colt's withers, asking Ending Shadows to run.

Shadows immediately launched into a fast gallop, pulling away from March to Honor. "Come on, Christina. Chase after me," Melanie murmured. March to Honor was faster than Shadows. It wouldn't be hard for them to catch up.

Melanie looked to her inside, where Christina and her horse had been. There was nothing. She kneaded her hands along her colt's neck. "Give me a little more, boy. Maybe your stablemate will decide to go after you even if Christina doesn't want him to."

Shadows picked up speed. A few seconds later Melanie glanced to her right again. There was still nothing. She looked up the track. They had less than a furlong to go. Perhaps Christina had tried to return to the track too soon.

"Eat our dust, Graham!"

Melanie whipped her head to the side. She saw March to Honor's neck. "Not a chance, Chris!" she shot back, tapping Shadows with her crop. She could barely keep herself from shouting out in happiness. The old Christina was back!

Shadows sped up gamely, but March to Honor was blazing. Christina's mount opened up a half-length lead, extending it to a full length as the horses blistered across the finish line.

"Great job, Chris," Melanie said when she and Shadows finally caught up.

"March to Honor did all the work. He kept fighting to run, even when I was scared," Christina replied. She leaned down, patting the horse's copper neck and praising him for his effort. "I think he and Charisma could both be Triple Crown contenders next year." She sat back up. "But it's probably too early to think about that. We just got through the last one, after all."

Melanie shrugged. "It's fun to dream big," she said. "How's your wrist?"

"It's fine." Christina smiled, the tension leaving her face. "I'm fine, too."

"Are you sure?"

Christina nodded. "I needed this breeze," she replied. "Don't tell Mom, but I almost lost it at the beginning."

"What happened?" Melanie was pretty sure she could guess Christina's answer.

"I kept feeling like I was falling. It was like March to Honor was stumbling with every stride that he took." Christina shuddered. "It took almost a furlong for me to make my body do what it was supposed to."

"I had the same problem after Image's accident," Melanie said. "Every time a horse's front leg hit the ground hard, I thought it would snap just like Image's did."

"How long did it take before you stopped being afraid?"

"I'm still afraid," Melanie admitted. "But maybe it will be different for you."

Christina shook her head. "I doubt that." She took a deep breath before adding, "We'd better get these horses back. I need to get on Matt for his final breeze before the Suburban."

Although the sky had been clear during the morning workouts, dark clouds had started appearing on the horizon as the races began. By late afternoon it was raining in earnest. Melanie eyed the downpour through the taxi window that evening, wishing she had brought an umbrella.

Jazz had called earlier in the afternoon. He was on his way to Europe with the band, but he had arranged for a long layover in New York and wanted to have dinner with Melanie.

Melanie paid the taxi driver and darted from the taxi to the overhang in front of the restaurant. Her choice of clothing for the evening, a black flowered dress and heeled sandals, was not appropriate for the rain, but she wanted to look nice for Jazz.

Jazz was waiting for her in the lobby. "You look beautiful," he said, kissing her.

"Actually, I look like a drowned rat, but thanks for ignoring that," Melanie replied. "You don't look half bad yourself." Jazz was wearing khaki pants and a maroon polo shirt.

"Thanks. Anyway, my flight was late, so I didn't call in time to make reservations. If you want to eat here, there's a thirty-minute wait. But I saw a pizza parlor across the street that looked pretty tempting."

Melanie smiled. "I'm starving. Let's go for pizza."

Twenty minutes later Melanie and Jazz were sitting at a corner table in the restaurant, grabbing slices from their extra-cheese pizza. They had caught up on the events of the past few days. Jazz told stories from his concerts in North Carolina and Maryland, while

Melanie talked about her races and how Christina was doing.

"I had a long chat with Brad Townsend today," Jazz said after Melanie had told him about the morning's workouts.

Melanie quickly swallowed her mouthful of pizza. "Why didn't you tell me sooner?"

Jazz raised his hand apologetically. "I knew that you would freak out once I mentioned it, and I wanted to hear about the rest of your life first."

Melanie put down her slice. "What's the news?"

"Dr. Dalton is happy with Image's progress. They're walking her for half an hour each day now," Jazz replied.

"Did he say anything about when we could move Image back to Whitebrook?"

"The consensus seems to be that she needs at least until the end of July." Jazz finished his slice of pizza. He wiped his hands before reaching across the table to take Melanie's.

Melanie could feel Jazz's hands tremble. "We already knew that. What aren't you telling me?"

"I've been going over the band's budget. Our ticket sales for this European tour have been lower than we expected." Jazz sighed. "And on top of that, when Brad gave me the newest total for Image's treatment, he told me that he's raising her board rates."

"He can't do that without giving you advance notice!" Melanie protested angrily.

"He's the farm's owner. He can do whatever he wants," Jazz said, looking away from her. "You know I'd do anything for Image, Mel, but I also have an obligation to the band. And I've reached a point where I have to either make compromises in Image's treatment or cancel some of the band's recording sessions while we're in Europe."

Melanie flinched when she heard this second option. She had seen Jazz in concert in Lexington, and she knew how much he loved everything about the band. Pegasus was Jazz's dream, just as training Image had been hers. She couldn't let Jazz make such a sacrifice. "There is a third choice."

Jazz nodded. He released Melanie's hands. "Brad brought it up when we talked today."

Melanie closed her eyes, remembering her ride on Enigmatic. The Johnstons had been so excited about that colt's potential, hoping he would show his sire's courage and power. She knew she would feel the same way when she sat on the back of Image's foals. But Image would have many foals. She could give Brad the first one.

"It's not what you think," Jazz said. "Brad did say that he would cover all the costs of Image's stay at Townsend Acres after the Kentucky Derby in exchange for full ownership of her first foal, but I turned him down."

Melanie opened her eyes. "Why? It would have solved all your financial problems."

"I can't stand the thought of anyone except you riding Image's foals." Jazz leaned across the table and kissed the top of Melanie's head.

Jazz's tender statement made warm tears spring to Melanie's eyes. She kissed Jazz back. "You have to call Brad and tell him you've changed your mind," she told him, forcing conviction into her voice. "Neither of the other options you mentioned is acceptable. Giving Brad Image's foal is the only way."

"No, I came up with another." Jazz took a deep breath. "I told Brad that I would pay half the bills, and in exchange for the other half, I would breed Image to Celtic Mist early next year and give him a half interest in the foal."

"I'm not sure that's the best idea, Jazz," Melanie replied reluctantly. "The Reeses had a similar arrangement with the Townsends for Wonder's foals. Ashleigh has told me so many horrible stories about the endless bickering that took place with horses like Wonder's Pride and Townsend Princess. Brad made it almost impossible for my aunt and uncle to do things in the horses' best interests. He did the same thing with Star before he sold his interest to Christina when the colt was so sick."

"I know that," Jazz said. "That's why I put some provisions in the agreement."

"What sorts of provisions?" Melanie couldn't imagine anything that would keep Brad from interfering.

"First, Brad gets only forty-nine percent ownership. I'll retain the other fifty-one percent, which gives me control in choosing a trainer. Also, I've written into the contract that you will be the horse's jockey." Jazz took Melanie's hands again. "It took some fast talking to get Brad to agree to this. But I managed to convince him that the potential revenue from his share of Image's first foal would more than cover my debts. I think this is the best deal I can make, Mel. If you don't like it, though, I'll think of something else."

Melanie gaped at Jazz. "You're Image's owner. Why do you need my approval?"

"Well, as a horse owner, I've come to appreciate the way you train and jockey horses. So I thought it was in my best interest to lock you into the future of Image's foals." Jazz winked. "And as your boyfriend, I know better than to sign important papers concerning your favorite horse without running them by you first." Jazz looked at Melanie, his expression losing its playfulness. "What do you think?"

Melanie was still worried that Brad would find ways to undermine this foal's training, just as he had undermined Star's. But she couldn't think of anything else that would be fair to Jazz and to Image. "You should sign the papers," she replied at last.

"Are you sure about that?" Jazz squeezed her hands.

Melanie nodded. "I'm sure," she said, squeezing back. "Just remember that I now have it in writing that I get to ride Image's first foal." She wished she could look two years into the future and see what a wonderful horse the breeding of Image and Celtic Mist would produce.

"Of course you do." Jazz's face relaxed into a relieved smile. "But in the meantime I have some money that was originally earmarked for Image's rehabilitation, and it's burning a hole in my pocket. I'm really thinking that another racehorse wouldn't be a bad investment."

"Racehorses are a bit of a risk, but they're a lot more fun than stocks and bonds," Melanie agreed.

"Then again, you don't risk getting kicked when you're loading stocks and bonds into a trailer." Jazz laughed. "There were a few times when I thought Image wouldn't make it to a race."

"I know," Melanie said. She could list at least a dozen trailering incidents that the headstrong filly had been involved in. She wondered if Image would pass her intelligence and spirit to her foals. She hoped so. Even if it made them more difficult to train, it would make them unstoppable on the track.

"Anyway, I've already secured you as the jockey of Image's first foal, but while we're waiting, I was wondering if you'd like to help me find and train my next investment."

When Jazz had brought this up to Melanie a week earlier, she had thought that staying in Kentucky and training another horse would limit her opportunities as a jockey. Now she was less worried about that, and she couldn't deny that she wanted to work with Jazz again. "I would love to, Jazz," she said.

"So we're going to revive the partnership?" Jazz asked. He raised his glass. "We should drink to this."

Melanie smiled. "Actually, I have a better idea." She reached across the table and handed a slice of pizza to Jazz. Then she picked up her own slice. Tapping her slice against Jazz's, she said, "To Image and to all the horses we work with in the future."

Jazz nodded, tapping his slice against hers. "And to us," he added.

They both took a bite of pizza, sealing their deal.

13

It had been raining continuously since Thursday afternoon, and by Saturday the track was a sloppy mess. Christina stared at the television gloomily, watching as the horses struggled through puddles and kicked up waves of mud. She didn't have much experience with off tracks, and the Johnstons had told her that Matt hated them.

"The latest weather report says that the rain should stop within the next couple of hours," Melanie said, sitting down beside Christina. "I really hope it does. Cindy is going to scratch Rush Street if it's still raining at post time. She doesn't want to take too many chances with his leg."

Christina kept her eyes on the monitor. Rush Street's suspensory ligament injury had been more serious than Callie's bowed tendon. It was too easy for her to picture the Tall Oaks colt going down on the track.

Actually, it was too easy for her to picture any horse going down. She had put on a brave face for the past couple of days, trying to convince everyone else that she was over Callie's death. But her composure was an unpolished sculpture. If anyone looked too closely, they could see the chisel marks.

Christina looked out the window, half hoping the rain would continue. If Rush Street was scratched, then Melanie would be free to ride Matter of Time. But by post time for the third race, the downpour had softened to a dull drizzle, and by the end of the fourth race, the sun had started to peek between the gray clouds.

"Want to play some pool?" Melanie asked while they waited for the start of the fifth race. Post time for the Suburban was just under two hours away.

"Sure," Christina replied, needing a distraction. Neither she nor Melanie had originally been very good at this game, but the hours they spent in the jockeys' lounge gave them plenty of chances to practice.

Melanie handed Christina one of the cue sticks that rested along the wall. It was scratched and worn from years of use.

"Do you want to break?" Melanie asked. She lined up the balls in the triangle, rearranging them with practiced ease.

Christina shook her head, her eyes on the monitor, as she automatically rubbed the tip of the cue stick with blue chalk. "No, you go ahead."

Melanie broke the balls cleanly, setting up an easy shot for Christina. Christina hit the solid blue two ball into the corner pocket, but from there the game went downhill for her. She was so nervous that she couldn't hold the cue stick steady, and as often as not she scratched or sank one of Melanie's balls. When Melanie won the game with a tricky shot of the eight ball into the side pocket, there were still four of Christina's solid balls on the table.

"Want to play again?" Melanie asked, taking the balls out of the pockets and rolling them onto the table.

"I don't think we have time," Christina replied, checking the clock. Less than an hour to post time. "I'm going to change."

Christina spent the next half hour in the women's locker room, trying to compose herself. She stared at her reflection in the mirror. She was wearing Dreamflight's green-and-white diamond-patterned silks, just as she had the previous Saturday, when Callie had gone down.

What had she been thinking? Even though everyone had convinced her that she wasn't solely responsible for Callie's death, she wasn't ready to face the track again. But it was too late for her to back down. People were counting on her.

Methodically Christina wrapped an Ace bandage around her wrist. Her wrist hadn't been giving her any trouble the last few days, but the doctor had suggested that she play it safe.

"Come on, Chris," Melanie said, sticking her head through the door. "It's time to go weigh in."

Dazedly Christina stood in line in front of the scale with the other jockeys for the Suburban. The weight assignment for Matt was 123 pounds. He would be carrying one of the heavier weights. Rush Street had only been assigned 118 pounds.

"So Dreamflight's letting the bug ride despite what happened last week," one of the jockeys commented snidely as Christina stepped onto the scale. Apprentice jockeys were sometimes referred to as "bugs" because in the programs an asterisk followed their names to denote their status.

"Yeah, I thought there was an inquiry that banned her from the track," another replied.

Christina nearly lost her grip on the saddle. She stared straight ahead as the steward inserted lead weights, not wanting to admit how much the comments had hurt.

"Hey, don't listen to them," Melanie said as Christina stepped off the scale.

"Yes, we've all had our share of accidents," Emilio Casados, the jockey who had ridden Celtic Mist in the Triple Crown, agreed.

Christina smiled at the two jockeys, grateful for

their support. But soon panic seized her when the call came for post time.

"I'm not ready," she whispered. Numbly Christina followed the other jockeys to the track. Her footsteps echoed ominously in the long, hollow tunnel.

Matter of Time was near the center of the walking ring. Aaron was holding the bay horse's reins, and Matt stamped and flagged his tail as Christina approached. For a moment Christina saw white spots dancing in front of her eyes, and she blinked frantically to clear them.

As she walked toward Matt Christina saw some of the other action in the walking ring. Melanie was talking with Cindy as Beckie, one of Tall Oaks' grooms, stood at Rush Street's head. Nearby, Emilio Casados was mounting Storm Rider, a big black horse that had recently won the Brooklyn Handicap.

Matt whinnied, and Christina automatically reached up to pet the horse. "Hey, boy," she whispered. Her throat had constricted to the point where it was hard to speak.

"Are you all right?" Aaron asked softly.

Christina nodded. "Matt and I are going to circle the field," she replied with a forced smile. Her entire body was shaking, telling her that she no longer belonged in Dreamflight's silks. "By the way, Aaron, I never got a chance to thank you for what you said on Tuesday. You were right about Callie. It just took me some time to listen."

"Don't mention it," Aaron said. "You'll return the favor sometime. We're going to be riding together all summer, right?"

Christina nodded again as Patrick gave her a leg up. Normally she barely needed any assistance, but that day she was so nervous that the trainer practically had to lift her into the saddle.

"I think we should change our strategy," Amanda told Christina as she put her right foot in the stirrup. "Matt normally likes to stay near the front in the first few furlongs, but there's too much early speed. I'm especially worried about that horse your cousin is riding."

"So do you want us to stay further back?" Christina asked, still trying to get a firm grip on the reins. They were dangling like ribbons between her fingers. The Johnstons had asked her to change a horse's running style before, wanting her to rate Callie at the beginning of a race instead of letting him run straight to the lead. The result had been disastrous. Christina closed her eyes. She couldn't start thinking about Callie now.

"Yes. It should also keep the mud from bothering him as much. You don't need to worry about falling back by twelve or so lengths because Matt has the speed to catch up down the stretch," Amanda said. "The track's been favoring closers today."

"Also, try to stay a little off the rail," Patrick added.

"It's a mess there. I saw two horses slip and nearly go down in the last race."

Christina bit her lip, glad she hadn't seen that race. She vowed not to make the same mistake with Matt that she had made with Callie. If she felt him slip, then she was going to pull him up. "I'll do my best," she managed to say. Out of the corner of her eye she saw the escort rider. It was time to go to the track.

"Good luck," Patrick said as the escort rider took Matt's reins from Aaron.

Christina stared between Matt's ears, trying to focus on the track. The dirt wavered for a moment, and she took a deep breath, forcing back the butterflies. The last time she had been so scared was during her first race on Star, when she had needed to place well in order to keep Brad Townsend from gaining the right to train her beloved horse. But during that race and again during the Triple Crown, the pressure had been to win. She had not worried that one of the races would cost Star his life.

The post parade seemed to pass too quickly. Before Christina knew it, she was circling Matt behind the gate, waiting for their turn to load.

"The horses are loading for the five-hundred-thousand-dollar Suburban Handicap." The same announcer that had called the Riva Ridge Breeders' Cup was calling this race. "The race will be a mile and a quarter. The stakes record of one minute fifty-five and two-fifths seconds was set by Foolish Pleasure in 1976."

Every race began with an announcement of the purse and the stakes record. However, as she heard the announcer's words, Christina could think only about how she had been there just a week earlier, trying to calm Callie as the other horses loaded.

She and Matt had drawn the fourth post position. Before Patrick's warning, she had planned to edge Matt as far inside as possible, but now she did not want to risk being caught against the rail. Perhaps she could just ask Matt to run straight ahead and then stay near the middle of the track. If she kept Matt off the pace, then there wouldn't be too many horses jostling him in the first furlongs.

Two attendants approached Matt, ready to load him into the gate. Matt backed up warily, just as Callie had the week before. Christina automatically put her legs against Matt's sides and mumbled reassuringly. Matt didn't listen. The horse reared, sending the attendants leaping out of the way.

"Come on, boy. It's okay," Christina said when all four of Matt's feet were on the ground again. Her voice was barely a whisper. "Don't be scared. You do this all the time."

The attendants grabbed Matt's reins again. A third one stood behind the horse, pushing him into the gate. Christina held on, bracing herself for Matt's protests. The horse tried to rear two more times, and his legs moved as though they were on springs. But the attendants were ultimately able to force him into the enclosure and slam the gate behind him.

Christina breathed a sigh of relief as Matt stood quivering in the gate. The horse pushed at the front of the gate with his nose and kicked out once before finally accepting the confinement.

"That's a good boy," Christina praised. "Now, I know you've won a ton of races, so you're going to have to help me today."

The attendants yelled, "One back," as they prepared to load Rush Street. Christina glanced at her cousin through the bars of the gate. Melanie was looking straight ahead, her attention firmly on the race.

As the crowd noise died down in preparation for the race, Christina tried to follow Melanie's example. She looked between Matt's dark, flickering ears and took another deep, shuddering breath. "Come on, Matt. Let's run a good race for Callie, all right?"

"And they're off!" The gates opened, and Matt was lunging forward before Christina could react. Instinct kept her balanced in the saddle as she and Matt surged into the middle of the pack. Mud pummeled them from all sides.

Matt shook his head, not liking the mud. The clumps were flying so hard and fast that by the end of the first furlong they had coated Christina's first pair of goggles. She reached up with one hand to peel this pair off. Luckily, Melanie had reminded her to wear several pairs in these conditions. The horse in front of them kicked another clump of mud back. It hit Matt squarely in the chest, and he shied sideways.

Christina lurched in the saddle as Matt temporarily lost his footing. She clutched at a handful of mane to keep her seat, then pulled back on the reins. Her heart leaped into her throat. She had been wrong to think she could be Matt's jockey in this race. "Easy, Matt," she said shakily between gritted teeth. She couldn't open her mouth too wide without getting a mouthful of mud. "It's not our day. You'll get another chance later."

Matt righted himself and kept galloping forward. He did not obey the restraint. Christina pulled back again, determined to stop him. She was not going to let Matt keep running on this track. Maybe the Johnstons and Matt's owner would reprimand her, but nothing was worth being responsible for another horse's death. She couldn't fail Matt the way she had failed Callie.

Matt snorted his frustration as the other horses passed him. He tugged on the reins as though he wanted to pull them from Christina's grasp. Christina tried to calm him with her hands and legs, but she felt frozen in the saddle. In front of her, horses were running through the sloppy track, occasionally slipping as they tried to position themselves for the stretch run.

Blood roared in Christina's ears, and the action suddenly seemed to be very separate from her. It was as though she were watching the race from a monitor in the jockeys' lounge. She could see the horses but could not do anything about what was happening.

"After a slow forty-nine-second half mile, it's Rush Street and Centurion vying for the lead. Storm Rider is right behind." The roaring in Christina's ears and the dull thuds of hooves in the mud muffled the announcer's words. "Far back, it's Matter of Time fifteen lengths off the lead."

When she heard Matt's name, the roaring sound in Christina's ears faded. She became aware of her surroundings again, feeling Matt's insistent pull on the reins and sensing the horse's frustration at being kept from running.

And for the first time in a week Christina stopped thinking about the Riva Ridge Breeders' Cup and instead remembered another recent race on this track: the Belmont Stakes. Star had broken badly, and the colt had been trapped behind a wall of horses. Christina had known from the power in Star's strides and the way he strained against the bit that her horse could win. She had let him.

Now she could feel the tense energy in Matt, another brilliant horse. But what good was all that power if she made him hold it in? Matt deserved the chance to win as much as Star had.

Christina looked up the track again. The horses were rounding another turn, and some seemed to struggle to keep their footing. The nightmarish image of a horse falling again entered her mind. She turned her attention back to Matt, forcing this image away.

Riding was as much about knowing when to let go as it was about knowing when to hold back. March to Honor had reminded Christina of that just two days before. Christina might not have held back in time for Callie, but keeping Matt from running was not going to fix that mistake.

Christina slid her hands down Matt's neck, giving him rein. The horse exploded forward, kicking up mud as he ran after the other horses. Christina's throat closed in panic. She tried to fight that emotion, picturing how beautiful Matt looked as he rounded the turn. His neck was arched, his mane and tail were fanned out in the wind, and his hooves were barely brushing the sloppy track as he was caught in the pure joy of running.

With that picture in her mind, Christina knew she couldn't give up on racing yet. She had many more of these moments to look forward to, especially with Star. Maybe the Johnstons wouldn't want her to ride for them again after her hesitation in this race, but there would be other opportunities.

Matt was blowing past the other horses now, releasing the speed that Christina had held back in the earlier furlongs. Christina barely had to steer him through the openings.

The mud was hitting them again, and clumps stung the unprotected areas of Christina's face. As they entered the homestretch Christina peeled back her second pair of goggles, bringing her down to her final pair. There were still three horses in front of them, a solid wall along the middle of the track. If she steered Matt to the outside, there would not be enough time for them to catch up. Their only chance was to shoot along the rail, the most treacherous part of the track.

Before Christina could make a decision, Matt jerked his head forward, seizing the bit in his teeth. He thrust his head toward the rail, charging into the gap.

Christina gasped as she almost lost her balance again. This time it wasn't because Matt was slipping. Instead the powerful movements of Matt's hindquarters were pushing her forward onto the horse's neck.

Christina grabbed a handful of Matt's mane, steadying herself. "Okay, have it your way," she mumbled, not caring if dirt got in her mouth. "Let's win it!" She tapped her heels on Matt's side, asking the horse to change leads. Matt did so without hesitation, giving his strides renewed power. Christina crouched lower in the saddle, urging her horse toward the finish line.

Christina's goggles were covered in mud now, and she could hardly see. It didn't matter. Matt was doing everything he could to take the lead. She rubbed her hands along Matt's neck, focusing on the rhythm of his accelerating strides. They crossed the line in a blanket finish with three other horses.

"It's too close to call! What an incredible finish to this year's Suburban Handicap!"

Christina rocked back on her heels, barely able to

believe that the race was over. Beneath her, Matt was slowing down, his breathing hard and fast. Christina leaned over his neck to praise him. "You did it, boy. You ran a great race in spite of my mistakes."

Christina took off her final pair of goggles, watching the other horses on the track as well as the cheering crowd. A few strides ahead, Melanie was slowing Rush Street. Her cousin grinned at her, giving her a thumbs-up. Christina returned the gesture as she glanced at the results board. The word *photo* was still flashing.

"This one's for you, Callie," Christina whispered, looking up at the cloudy sky. But this moment wasn't Callie's alone. It also belonged to everyone who had helped her through this difficult week, giving her the strength to race again. And most importantly, it belonged to Matt, who had helped her remember what horse racing was all about.

The roar of the crowd made Christina turn her attention back to the board. Storm Rider had won. Rush Street had finished second. Matt's name and number were in the third spot.

Christina felt a pang of disappointment. She and Matt could have won if she had just given the horse his head a fraction of a second earlier.

But then Christina remembered what Dr. Reuter had told her when she visited the surgery clinic. Every race was a combination of circumstances. At that moment all the jockeys were probably considering what they could have done to tilt the circumstances in their favor. Yet this one race would not define any of their careers. All it did was teach them lessons that they would use when they rode in their next race.

As Christina trotted Matt off the track she thought about all the lessons she had learned since arriving at Belmont. Star had taught her the value of believing in her dreams, while Callie had shown her how easily dreams could be broken. And that day Matt had helped her take the first step toward recovering from these broken dreams.

There would undoubtedly be other lessons in the future. Christina smiled, glad she would have time to learn them.

Jockey Chris Antley, *center,* aboard Charismatic
signals his win after crossing the finish line to
capture the 125th running of the Kentucky
Derby, Saturday, May 1, 1999, in Louisville,
Kentucky. (AP Photo/Al Berhman)

CHARISMATIC

Unlike most Derby contenders, Charismatic began his three-year-old year in the claiming ranks. As late as February 11, 1999, anyone could have claimed him for $62,500. When Charismatic won the Kentucky Derby by a neck, the colt's trainer, D. Wayne Lukas, said that never in his training career had he misjudged a horse as he did this one.

In 1999 it had been over twenty years since any horse had won the Triple Crown. Racing fans thought they had a true contender in Charismatic. He won the Derby and the Preakness, and led down the homestretch in the Belmont Stakes before faltering and finishing third. About fifty yards past the wire, jockey Chris Antley jumped from Charismatic's back and cradled the colt's left front leg. X rays later showed that Charismatic had suffered condylar and sesamoid fractures, injuries that ended his racing career but fortunately did not threaten his life. Charismatic finished his career with five wins in seventeen starts, winning over $2 million and gaining the title of 1999 Horse of the Year. Charismatic was retired to stud, and his first crop of foals began racing in 2003.

Jennifer Chu grew up reading every horse book she could get her hands on and has been a fan of the Thoroughbred series since she was twelve years old. She recently graduated from Stanford University, where she spent most of her free time riding both English and Western for the Stanford Equestrian Team and competing on the Intercollegiate Horse Show Association circuit. She plans to continue riding as a medical student at Washington University in St. Louis. This is her second novel for young adults.

WIN A FREE RIDING SADDLE!

ENTER THE
THOROUGHBRED RIDING SADDLE
SWEEPSTAKES!

COMPLETE THIS ENTRY FORM • NO PURCHASE NECESSARY

NAME: _____

ADDRESS: _____

CITY: _____ STATE: _____ ZIP: _____

PHONE: _____ AGE: _____

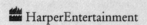

MAIL TO: THOROUGHBRED RIDING SADDLE SWEEPSTAKES!
c/o HarperCollins, Attn.: Department AW
10 E. 53rd Street   New York, NY 10022

HarperEntertainment

17th Street Productions,
an Alloy Online, Inc., company

THOROUGHBRED 60 SWEEPSTAKES RULES

────────────────── OFFICIAL RULES ──────────────────

1. No purchase necessary.

2. To enter, complete the official entry form or hand print your name, address, and phone number along with the words "Thoroughbred Riding Saddle Sweepstakes" on a 3" x 5" card and mail to: HarperCollins, Attn.: Department AW, 10 E. 53rd Street, New York, NY 10022. Entries must be received by October 1, 2003. Enter as often as you wish, but each entry must be mailed separately. One entry per envelope. Partially completed, illegible, or mechanically reproduced entries will not be accepted. Sponsors are not responsible for lost, late, mutilated, illegible, stolen, postage due, incomplete, or misdirected entries. All entries become the property of HarperCollins and will not be returned.

3. Sweepstakes open to all legal residents of the United States (excluding residents of Colorado and Rhode Island) who are between the ages of eight and

sixteen by October 1, 2003, excluding employees and immediate family members of HarperCollins, Alloy, Inc., or 17th Street Productions, an Alloy company, and their respective subsidiaries, and affiliates, officers, directors, shareholders, employees, agents, attorneys, and other representatives (individually and collectively), and their respective parent companies, affiliates, subsidiaries, advertising, promotion and fulfillments agencies, and the persons with whom each of the above are domiciled. Offer void where prohibited or restricted.

4. Odds of winning depend on total number of entries received. Approximately 100,000 entry forms distributed. All prizes will be awarded. Winners will be randomly drawn on or about October 15, 2003, by representatives of Harper-Collins, whose decisions are final. Potential winners will be notified by mail and a parent or guardian of the potential winner will be required to sign and return an affadavit of eligibility and release of liability within 14 days of notification. Failure to return affadavit within the specified time period will disqualify winner and another winner will be chosen. By acceptance of prize, winner consents to the use of his or her name, photographs, likeness, and personal information by HarperCollins, Alloy, Inc., and 17th Street Productions, an Alloy company, for publicity and advertising purposes without further compensation except where prohibited.

5. One (1) Grand Prize Winner will receive a Thoroughbred riding saddle. HarperCollins reserves the right at its sole discretion to substitute another prize of equal or of greater value in the event prize is unavailable. Approximate retail value $500.00.

6. Only one prize will be awarded per individual, family, or household. Prizes are nontransferable and cannot be sold or redeemed for cash. No cash substitute is available except at the sole discretion of HarperCollins for reasons of prize unavailability. Any federal, state, or local taxes are the responsibility of the winner.

7. Additional terms: By participating, entrants agree a) to the official rules and decisions of the judges which will be final in all respects; and b) to release, discharge, and hold harmless HarperCollins, Alloy Online, Inc., and 17th Street Productions, an Alloy Online, Inc., company, and their affiliates, subsidiaries, and advertising promotion agencies from and against any and all liability or damages associated with acceptance, use, or misuse of any prize received in this sweepstakes.

8. To obtain the name of the winner, please send your request and a self-addressed stamped envelope (Vermont residents may omit return postage) to "Thoroughbred Riding Saddle Winners List," c/o HarperCollins, Attn: Department AW, 10 E. 53rd Street, New York, NY 10022.

SPONSOR: HarperCollins Publishers Inc.